P9-CRH-122

"All I Ever Dreamed Of Was Having A Home.

"Stability. Roots. But you didn't want those same things, Pete. That's why I had to end it."

He took a step toward Carol, then stopped, thinning his lips. "Do you want me to tell you that I've changed?" he growled. "That I want a wife and a family? Well, I haven't changed. I'm still Pete Dugan," he said, and thumped an angry fist against his chest.

Carol lifted her chin in defiance. "Looks like you'll never be anything more than a good-time man, chasing from one rodeo to the next, whooping it up and turning every day into a cowboy Saturday night."

Scowling, Pete flung an impatient hand at her and turned away. "Go home, Carol. Back to your house and the roots you want so badly. I'm not the man for you. I never was."

So why did he have to tamp down his instincts to block her exit, to take her into his arms, when she headed for the door...?

Dear Reader,

This Fourth of July, join in the fireworks of Silhouette's 20th anniversary year by reading all six powerful, passionate, provocative love stories from Silhouette Desire!

July's MAN OF THE MONTH is a *Bachelor Doctor* by Barbara Boswell. Sparks ignite when a dedicated doctor discovers his passion for his loyal nurse!

With *Midnight Fantasy,* beloved author Ann Major launches an exciting new promotion in Desire called BODY & SOUL. Our BODY & SOUL books are among the most sensuous and emotionally intense you'll ever read. Every woman wants to be loved…BODY & SOUL, and in these books you'll find a heady combination of breathtaking love and tumultuous desire.

Amy J. Fetzer continues her popular WIFE, INC. miniseries with *Wife for Hire.* Enjoy *Ride a Wild Heart,* the first sexy installment of Peggy Moreland's miniseries TEXAS GROOMS. This month, Desire offers you a terrific two-books-in-one value—*Blood Brothers* by Anne McAllister and Lucy Gordon. A British lord and an American cowboy are look-alike cousins who switch lives temporarily…and lose their hearts for good in this romance equivalent of a doubleheader. And don't miss the debut of Kristi Gold, with her moving love story *Cowboy for Keeps*—it's a keeper!

So make your summer sizzle—treat yourself to all six of these sultry Desire romances!

Happy Reading!

Joan Marlow Golan

Joan Marlow Golan
Senior Editor, Silhouette Desire

Please address questions and book requests to:
Silhouette Reader Service
U.S.: 3010 Walden Ave., P.O. Box 1325, Buffalo, NY 14269
Canadian: P.O. Box 609, Fort Erie, Ont. L2A 5X3

Ride a Wild Heart

PEGGY MORELAND

Silhouette® Desire®

Published by Silhouette Books

America's Publisher of Contemporary Romance

If you purchased this book without a cover you should be aware
that this book is stolen property. It was reported as "unsold and
destroyed" to the publisher, and neither the author nor the
publisher has received any payment for this "stripped book."

In memory of Tommy Wilson McCarley,
January 27, 1952–February 7, 1971.
A true cowboy and a gentleman…and my first true love.

A special thanks to bronc rider Travis Ring
for answering a zillion questions about rodeos and bronc riding.
Your willingness to share information
is a testament to the Cowboy Code.

 SILHOUETTE BOOKS

ISBN 0-373-76306-9

RIDE A WILD HEART

Copyright © 2000 by Peggy Bozeman Morse

All rights reserved. Except for use in any review, the reproduction
or utilization of this work in whole or in part in any form by any
electronic, mechanical or other means, now known or hereafter
invented, including xerography, photocopying and recording, or in
any information storage or retrieval system, is forbidden without
the written permission of the editorial office, Silhouette Books,
300 East 42nd Street, New York, NY 10017 U.S.A.

All characters in this book have no existence outside the imagination of
the author and have no relation whatsoever to anyone bearing the same
name or names. They are not even distantly inspired by any individual
known or unknown to the author, and all incidents are pure invention.

This edition published by arrangement with Harlequin Books S.A.

® and TM are trademarks of Harlequin Books S.A., used under license.
Trademarks indicated with ® are registered in the United States Patent
and Trademark Office, the Canadian Trade Marks Office and in other
countries.

Visit Silhouette at www.eHarlequin.com

Printed in U.S.A.

Books by Peggy Moreland

Silhouette Desire

A Little Bit Country #515
Run for the Roses #598
Miss Prim #682
The Rescuer #765
Seven Year Itch #837
The Baby Doctor #867
Miss Lizzy's Legacy #921
A Willful Marriage #1024
*Marry Me, Cowboy #1084
*A Little Texas Two-Step #1090
*Lone Star Kind of Man #1096
†The Rancher's Spittin' Image #1156
†The Restless Virgin #1163
†A Sparkle in the Cowboy's Eyes #1168
†That McCloud Woman #1227
**Billionaire Bridegroom #1244
†Hard Lovin' Man #1270
‡Ride a Wild Heart #1306

Silhouette Special Edition

Rugrats and Rawhide #1084

*Trouble in Texas
†Texas Brides
**Texas Cattleman's Club
‡Texas Grooms

PEGGY MORELAND

published her first romance with Silhouette in 1989. She's a natural storyteller with a sense of humor that will tickle your fancy, and Peggy's goal is to write a story that readers will remember long after the last page is turned. Winner of the 1992 National Readers' Choice Award, and a 1994 RITA finalist, Peggy frequently appears on best-seller lists around the country. A native Texan, she and her family live in Round Rock, Texas.

IT'S OUR 20th ANNIVERSARY!
We'll be celebrating all year,
Continuing with these fabulous titles,
On sale in July 2000.

Intimate Moments

 #1015 Egan Cassidy's Kid
Beverly Barton

 #1016 Mission: Irresistible
Sharon Sala

 #1017 The Once and Future Father
Marie Ferrarella

#1018 Imminent Danger
Carla Cassidy

MMM #1019 The Detective's Undoing
Jill Shalvis

#1020 Who's Been Sleeping in Her Bed?
Pamela Dalton

Special Edition

#1333 The Pint-Sized Secret
Sherryl Woods

 #1334 Man of Passion
Lindsay McKenna

#1335 Whose Baby Is This?
Patricia Thayer

#1336 Married to a Stranger
Allison Leigh

#1337 Doctor and the Debutante
Pat Warren

#1338 Maternal Instincts
Beth Henderson

Desire

 #1303 Bachelor Doctor
Barbara Boswell

#1304 Midnight Fantasy
Ann Major

#1305 Wife for Hire
Amy J. Fetzer

 #1306 Ride a Wild Heart
Peggy Moreland

#1307 Blood Brothers
Anne McAllister & Lucy Gordon

#1308 Cowboy for Keeps
Kristi Gold

Romance

 #1456 Falling for Grace
Stella Bagwell

 #1457 The Borrowed Groom
Judy Christenberry

#1458 Denim & Diamond
Moyra Tarling

#1459 The Monarch's Son
Valerie Parv

 #1460 Jodie's Mail-Order Man
Julianna Morris

#1461 Lassoed!
Martha Shields

One

There were times in a cowboy's life when eight seconds seemed like a lifetime.

For Pete Dugan those times were few and far between.

Not that he considered himself any more talented than the other bronc riders he competed against, nor did he feel he had more nerve. He just loved rodeoing. The lights, the crowds, the sleepless nights on the road chasing from one town to the next, the people, the camaraderie. The thrill of climbing onto the back of a mean-tempered bronc.

And this rodeo was no different from any other. Country music pulsed from a state-of-the-art sound system, while cowboys milled behind the chutes, shooting the breeze and joking around, passing the time until it was their turn to compete. The air all but crackled with the energy created by wired nerves and was thick with dueling scents—some enticing and drifting from the concession area, others earthy and familiar and associated with the roughstock penned behind the chutes.

Feeling the rush of adrenaline that every ride drew, Pete hitched a boot high on a rail of the chute and pulled himself up to look out over the rodeo arena. Dust thickened the air around the chutes, churned by the livestock, but through it Pete had a fair view of the filled stands.

A full house, he thought, and began to smile. And a noisy one. He liked that. Crowds made some cowboys nervous, but not Pete. He liked playing to a full house. And he liked his broncs full, too…electric, even a little rank.

The blue roan he'd drawn for the Mesquite Championship Rodeo was just such an animal, a high roller who shot straight up in the air right out of the chute and continued that sky-high bucking throughout the eight-second ride. Though Pete knew the horse he'd drawn, Diablo, would score high with the judges, he also knew the remainder of the points were his to earn.

"Ready?"

Pete turned to grin at the chute boss. "Always."

He gave the leather strap on his resined glove a yank, tightening it around his wrist, then leaned over the railing to check the tension on his rigging's cinch. Satisfied, he swung a leg over the chute, bracing his feet on the railings and his body above the horse, then slowly eased down over the bronc's back. He felt the horse blow up beneath him, bowing

his back, and knew without a doubt that the roan
would be airborne the minute the gate opened.

And Pete was ready to fly.

He jammed his Resistol down over his ears, then
leaned way back, curling his gloved fingers tightly
around the handle of the rigging. He could feel the
heat of the resin working, holding his gloved fingers
in place. Drawing his knees up, he positioned his
spurs high on the horse's shoulders, then jerked his
chin, signaling he was ready to ride.

The gate swung wide and the horse spun for the
opening, looking for freedom…he found it one step
out into the arena. He leaped high, then kicked out,
throwing his rump hard against Pete's spine. Muscles burned, and ligaments, already stretched and
torn, took another beating as eleven hundred pounds
of horsepower hit the end of the hand Pete gripped
on the rigging.

He set his jaw against the pain and searched for
the rhythm. It was there waiting for him, as familiar
as a lover's dance. With his spine almost level with
the roan's broad back, he focused on the timing,
drawing his knees high and his toes out, spurring in
sync with the bronc's wild bucks, while whipping
his free hand through the air above his head to keep
his hips centered in the swell with each of the
horse's sudden twists and turns. He heard the loud
cheers coming from the stands and knew the fans
were getting their money's worth.

Diablo was putting on one hell of a show.

And Pete Dugan wasn't doing too badly himself.

Sweat stung his eyes, and the muscles in his legs
and arms felt as if they were on fire. But Pete was

confident that, if necessary, he could ride that bronc all night. Through the roar in his ears, he heard the buzzer sound, signaling the end of his eight-second ride. Cheers rose from the stands, and the grin that was as much a part of Pete's features as his Roman-shaped nose quickly spread to his ears.

Working his gloved fingers loose in the rigging, he glanced to his left, looking for the pickup man. Just as he did, the roan spun sharply, slamming Pete's right leg up hard against the arena wall. He heard the collective gasp that rose from the stands even as the pain shot from his knee and up his thigh like a bolt of white-hot lightning, making his stomach churn and his head swim. Clenching his teeth against the dizziness, he made a grab for the arena wall and hung on, letting the roan run out from beneath him.

Gasping, nearly blinded by pain, he glanced up at the faces peering down at him from over the top rail that framed the box seats. His gaze struck a pair of green eyes centered on his. The eyes, filled with concern, were achingly familiar.

Carol?

It couldn't be, he told himself. He hadn't seen or heard from her in over two years. He closed his eyes and gave his head a shake, sure that he was hallucinating, a result of the pain. When he opened them, she was gone.

"Eighty-nine points!" the rodeo announcer called out. "Let's hear it for Pete Dugan, rodeo fans. This cowboy's just broken the record for the highest score ever made in the bronc riding event at the Mesquite Rodeo."

Loosening his grip on the wall, Pete dropped to the ground, hopping three steps until he was sure his right knee was going to take his weight. When he was sure he wasn't going to crumple like a rag doll and humiliate himself in front of over a thousand rodeo fans, he planted both boots firmly in the dirt and ripped off his hat. With a loud whoop, he sailed it high in the air and punched the air with his fists.

The audience went wild.

Grinning, Pete stooped to pick up his hat, then waved it over his head in a salute to the crowd before settling it back over his sweat-creased hair and limping his way back to the chutes.

"You okay?"

Pete waved away the medic. "Yeah, I'm all right." To prove it, he planted a boot on the fence rail and hauled himself to the top, then swung a leg over and dropped down on the other side. He landed beside his traveling buddy, Troy Jacobs.

"Helluva ride," Troy said with a nod toward the giant screen where the ride was being replayed.

"Yep," Pete agreed. "That Diablo sure knows how to raise some dust." He glanced back over his shoulder at the computerized scoreboard and added, "But Ty Murrey's up next. We'll have to wait and see if my score will hold."

"He'll give you a run for the money. No doubt about that. But your score'll hold," Troy assured him, watching the screen as the chute swung open for Ty Murrey's ride.

Pete turned his back on the rodeo arena and the giant screen that offered the rodeo fans a live and up-close view of the action going on in the arena.

The same as every other cowboy on the circuit, Pete had his superstitions and rituals that he adhered to religiously, and one of them was to never, ever watch the next competitor out of the box after his own ride. Instead, he caught between his teeth the strip of leather that bound his wrist and gave it a tug, loosening it as he glanced back up at the section of box seats where he thought he'd seen Carol. As he pulled off his glove, he swept his gaze across the sea of faces, looking for a woman with flaming red hair and green eyes.

Telling himself he was a fool for even looking, he started to turn away but whipped back when the crowd shifted, revealing the woman he'd seen while hanging from the arena wall. Her gaze met his, and he froze, his heart freezing, too.

Carol. It was Carol.

With his heart a dead, aching weight in his chest, he tucked his glove into the belt of his chaps and started toward the rail, his gaze locked on hers. He hadn't taken more than two steps when she bolted from her seat and fled up the ramp, disappearing into the crowd.

Pete stared, anger pulsing through him. He debated his chances of finding her in the crowd, then whirled away, ripping off his hat. Swearing, he slapped it against his chaps, making dust fly.

He wouldn't chase after her. Not Pete Dugan. Not when she'd left him high and dry more than two years before.

Haunted by the image of Carol, but determined not to waste his time thinking about her, Pete strode straight for the bar, his spurs jingling on the planked wood floor. "Beer's on me!" he yelled and dropped his duffel bag with his bronc riding gear at his feet.

Upon hearing the call for free beer, cowboys crowded up behind him.

Pete slapped a hand on the bar. "Line 'em up, bartender." He swelled his chest a bit and gave it a smug rub, grinning. "We've got us some celebrating to do."

Pitchers were quickly filled and placed on the bar, thick white foam spilling over their sides and pooling on the bar's scarred surface.

"What are you celebrating, cowboy?"

Pete glanced over at the woman who pressed herself against his side, and gave her a slow, appreciative look up and down. A smile built as he decided that this little buckle bunny might be just the distraction he needed to take his mind off Carol. "Well, darlin'—" But before he could tell her about the bronc riding record he'd just broken, one of the cowboys picked up a pitcher of beer and dumped it over Pete's head while the other men looking on cheered and hooted.

Pete yelped as the icy beer sluiced over the brim of his hat and down his back, then gave a loud whoop and ripped off his hat, tossing it high in the air. "Let the good times roll!"

Grabbing the woman around the waist, he danced her a fast waltz around the room, keeping time with the country song currently blaring from the jukebox. He stumbled to a stop when a wide hand closed over his shoulder from behind.

"Pete?"

Dragging a sleeve across his eyes to swipe at the beer that still dripped from his forehead, he turned to find Troy standing behind him. He shrugged off his friend's hand. "Not now, Troy. Can't you see I'm busy? Me and—" he peered down at the woman, frowning "—what did you say your name was, darlin'?"

She smiled up at him and sidled closer, rubbing her abdomen against his belt buckle. "Cheyenne."

Pete grinned and did some belt polishing of his own as he told Troy, "Me and Cheyenne are dancing."

"Clayton left."

Pete whipped his head around, his eyebrows snapping together over his brow, his grin disappearing. "Left? Where'd he go?"

"Rena called."

Noticing for the first time the worried look on his buddy's face, Pete dropped a quick, if distracted, kiss on the woman's mouth. "Stay right there, darlin'. This won't take but a minute." Taking Troy by the elbow, he herded his friend toward the empty hall where the restrooms were located and the noise level was somewhat less. "What's the problem?"

"She's gone."

Confused, Pete furrowed his brow. "Rena?"

"Yeah," Troy confirmed with a sigh. "She's left Clayton. Packed up the kids and went to her mother's."

"Oh, man," Pete said, swiping a shaky hand across his forehead. "That's a shame. When did this happen?"

"About an hour ago. She called and left a mes-

sage on his cell phone. He's already gone. Hitched
a ride with one of the boys who was headed for
Austin. Said he needed to check on the ranch and
pick up his truck. He wants you and me to take care
of his ranch while he's gone.'' Troy sighed again,
hooking his thumbs through his belt loops. ''Problem is, I've already promised Yuma I'd haze for him
at a rodeo in New Mexico.''

Pete mentally rearranged his schedule. ''Don't
worry. I can handle things alone.''

Troy looked at him uncertainly. ''You sure?''

Pete reared back, bracing his hands low on his
hips. ''Who the hell do you think you're talking to?
Some greenhorn?'' He swelled his chest and
thumped a fist against it. ''This here is Pete Dugan,
current contender for World Champion Bronc Rider.
I believe I ought to be able to handle a little old
ranch by myself for a couple of days.''

''I know Clayton wouldn't ask if he wasn't desperate,'' Troy said, still looking uncertain. ''He said
his hired hand's home with the chicken pox. Caught
it from his kids. He tried calling Carol, but she
wasn't home.''

At the mention of Carol, Pete sagged against the
wall. No, Carol wasn't home, he thought, swallowing hard. She was right here in Mesquite at the
rodeo. He'd seen her himself less than two hours
before. ''Carol still leases that place down the road
from Clayton's?'' he asked uneasily.

''Yeah. And she teaches riding lessons a couple
of times a week in his arena. Is that going to be a
problem for you?''

Pete dropped his head back against the wall and

stared up at the shadowed ceiling. "No," he said, trying to convince himself it was true. "No problem."

"How soon can you leave? Clayton said he'd wait until you got there."

"Three hours, max."

It was nearly two in the morning when Pete bumped his way across the cattle guard marking the entrance to Clayton's ranch. His eyes gritty from lack of sleep, he dragged a hand down his face and sighed. Ahead he could see the porch light was on...and Clayton on the top step, pacing.

Though Pete knew he'd miss a rodeo or two by filling in for Clayton, he figured if his efforts helped his friend save his marriage, the sacrifice was well worth any loss he might suffer in the standings. Both Clayton and Troy were his buddies, traveling the rodeo circuit with him, and, for all practical purposes, the only family he had.

Forcing an overbright smile for Clayton's benefit, he hopped down from the truck. "The troops have arrived!" he shouted, then felt his knee give way beneath him. Cursing, he stumbled, but quickly righted himself.

"You're drunk," Clayton said, his eyes narrowing.

Pete straightened indignantly. "I am not."

Clayton stepped closer, sniffing. Curling his nose, he withdrew. "You smell like a damn brewery. How the hell am I supposed to leave my ranch in the hands of a drunk?"

Angered by his friend's wrongful assumption,

Pete tossed back, "Well, you sure as hell didn't seem to mind leaving your ranch in a woman's hands for the past three years."

Clayton whirled, his eyes dark with warning. "My marriage is none of your business."

Pete took a step toward him, ready to argue the point, but stumbled again when his knee buckled a second time. He sucked in a breath as pain shot up his leg. Setting his jaw, he bent at the waist and gripped his hands above his knee caps, trying to swallow back the nausea that rose.

"You *are* drunk," Clayton accused angrily.

Before Pete could offer another denial, Clayton ducked a shoulder into his midsection, picked him up fireman-style and strode for the corral.

"Put me down, dammit!" Pete yelled. "I'm *not* drunk!"

"You won't be in a minute." With no more warning than that, Clayton heaved Pete from his shoulder and dumped him in the horse trough.

Pete came up sputtering, scraping the water from his eyes. He glared up at Clayton. "You jackass! I'm not drunk! It's my knee, dammit!" He fished his cowboy hat from the murky water and levered himself from the trough. His shirt and jeans were plastered to his body, and water sluiced down his face and dripped from his chin.

"Your knee?" Clayton dropped his gaze to stare at the bandage wrapped tightly around his friend's leg.

Pete slapped the waterlogged hat over his head. "Yes, my knee. The bronc I rode last night thought the pickup man was taking a little too long in fetching me, so he decided to scrape me off his back on the arena wall. Wrenched my bad knee.''

Clayton ducked his head. ''I didn't know.''

''No, you didn't. You just assumed. And you know what happens when a person *assumes* something, don't you?''

Scowling, Clayton glanced up. Then, heaving a sigh, he slung an arm around his friend's shoulders and headed him back toward the house. ''Yeah. He makes an ass of himself,'' he muttered.

''Apology accepted.''

Clayton whipped his head around to frown at Pete. ''I didn't offer an apology.''

Pete grinned and looped his arm over Clayton's shoulders, letting his friend take most of his weight. ''No, but I could tell you wanted to.'' His grin widened while Clayton's frown deepened. Limping along at his friend's side, Pete felt the water squishing inside his boots and figured they were ruined...but decided he'd take that up with Clayton later. His buddy had enough on his mind at the moment. ''You packed and ready to go?''

''Yeah.''

''How long will you be gone?''

''Long as it takes.''

''You gonna put up a fight for her?''

At the porch Clayton dropped his arm from Pete's shoulders and turned to face him. ''If that's what's required.''

''She's worth it,'' Pete said with a nod of approval. ''Rena's a good woman.''

Clayton glanced toward the house, his expression unreadable in the darkness. ''Yeah. I suppose.''

Heaving a weighty sigh, he stooped and picked up his duffel bag. "Are you sure you can handle the ranch alone?"

Pete smiled confidently. "Don't worry about a thing."

With a last, doubtful look, Clayton turned for his truck. "I left a list of instructions on the kitchen table. If you need me, you can reach me on my cell phone."

"You just bring Rena and the kids back home where they belong," Pete called after him. "I'll take care of things here." He lifted a hand in farewell, then, when he was sure Clayton couldn't see the action, he sank down on the porch step with a groan. He stretched out his leg to relieve the pressure on his throbbing knee...and wondered how he was going to manage a fifteen-hundred-acre ranch when the thought of making the short trek to his truck to gather his gear filled him with dread.

Pete awakened to pain. But that was nothing new. Seemed pain was his constant companion. He rolled to his back, his hand going instinctively to the puckered flesh on his knee. The scar his fingers rubbed at was two years old, left by a surgeon's knife, but the pain in his knee wasn't old. It was constant. He'd learned to live with it, as he had another pain...the one in his heart.

Refusing to think about that other pain, or the woman who had caused it, he pushed himself to a sitting position. He swung his left leg over the side of the bed and gingerly guided his right leg to join it. Standing, he kept his weight on his good leg as he tested the strength in the right. When it wobbled, he sighed and reached for the bandage he'd tossed over the chair the night before and sank back down on the bed, knowing he wouldn't make it very far without the added support. He wrapped the knee tightly, then stood again, testing his knee's ability to take his weight. Satisfied that it could, he tugged on his blue jeans and reached for his shirt. Barefoot, he limped for the kitchen. His boots were by the back door, where he'd left them, and a pool of water lay beneath the ruined leather soles. And, dangit, they were his favorite pair, too.

"You owe me a new pair of boots, Clayton," he muttered as he detoured for the coffeemaker. He reached for the can of grounds and caught a glimpse of his hat lying on the counter, its brim limp, its crown crushed. "And a hat," he added, frowning as he measured grounds into the basket. While the coffee perked, he hopscotched his way across the rocky drive to his truck and dug out an old pair of boots from behind the seat. Grabbing his cellular phone from the base unit on the console, he stuck it in his shirt pocket.

As he turned to head back to the house, he saw a truck by the barn...and stopped, staring, his heart slowly sinking to his stomach. He knew who the truck belonged to. And knew, too, that he might as well get it over with. No sense in avoiding the inevitable.

Bending over, he quickly stuck a foot into a boot, pulled it on, then gritted his teeth as he hopped a full circle, struggling to tug on the other one. Winded by the exertion, he straightened, hitching his hands low on his hips, and stared in the direction of the barn, dreading the confrontation.

But he had to do it, he told himself. There was no way he was going to be able to avoid seeing her, short of leaving Clayton in a bind.

Setting his jaw, he headed for the barn, trying to hide his limp, just in case she was watching. A man had his pride, after all, he reminded himself. He stepped inside the dim interior and paused, letting his eyes adjust to the sudden change in light. He heard her murmuring softly to a horse in the far stall. As the sound of her voice washed over him, he curled his hands into tight fists at his sides. God, how he'd missed her.

But he wouldn't let her know. Not when she had left him high and dry, without a word of explanation.

Hoping to keep his presence unknown for as long as possible, he followed the sound of her voice, keeping his tread light as he moved down the long alleyway. At the stall where she worked, he moved to the gate and braced his hands along its top rail. Inside, she was bent over, cleaning clods of dirt and stone from a sorrel mare's rear hoof. Worn jeans covered long legs, slightly bent, and hugged slim hips shaped like an upside-down heart. A bright yellow T-shirt stretched across her back and was tucked neatly into the waist of her jeans. The brim of a stained cap shadowed her face, and hair—nearly the same shade of red as the mare's sleek coat—spilled like a waterfall from the cap's back opening and over her shoulders.

At the sight of her his chest tightened painfully.

"Hello, Carol."

She dropped the mare's hoof and whirled. He watched her green eyes widen and was glad that he'd had the element of surprise on his side. If the situation had been reversed and she'd walked up on him unsuspected, he was afraid he might have fainted dead away. Or cried. And he wasn't sure which would've been worse.

Her eyes slowly narrowed and she turned her back to him, stooping to lift the mare's hoof again.

"Hello, Pete."

"Saw you at the rodeo last night. Were you there to watch me ride?"

She tossed a frown over her shoulder. "In your dreams, maybe." Turning her attention back to the horse's hoof, she added, "If you're looking for Clayton, he's not here."

Though her comment stung, Pete hadn't expected any less from her. She'd made it clear two years ago that she didn't want to see him again. But what she hadn't made clear was why. "I didn't come to see Clayton. I came to take care of the place while he goes chasing after Rena."

"He's wasting his time."

Pete opened the gate and stepped inside, closing it behind him. "What makes you say that?"

"Rena finally wised up and realized that Clayton doesn't want a wife."

"He married her, didn't he?"

She dropped the mare's hoof and slowly turned to face him. "Only because he had to." She tossed the hoof pick into the tack box and retrieved a brush.

Placing a hand on the mare's wide rump, she moved to the animal's opposite side.

Pete watched her, wondering if she felt she needed the barrier of the horse between them. "Clayton didn't *have* to do anything. He married Rena because he wanted to."

She snorted a laugh as she swept the brush along the mare's neck. "Uh-huh. And I'm sure that's why he stays on the road all the time, seldom coming home and rarely bothering to call to check on his wife and kids."

He knew what she said was true. Hadn't he worried about the same thing, constantly nagging at Clayton to call Rena and let her know that he was all right? Still, he felt an obligation to defend his friend. "You know what life's like on the circuit. Racing from one rodeo to the next. Operating on little or no sleep. Eating breakfast in one state, dinner in another."

She stopped brushing and lifted her head, focusing in on the cell phone he'd tucked in his shirt pocket. Slowly she lifted her gaze to his, arching a brow. "You know, technology is a wondrous thing. A person can pick up a phone and make a call no matter what the time or their location." She gave her head a shake and went back to her brushing. "Sorry, Pete. Can't buy into that excuse."

He tossed his hands up in frustration. "Okay, so maybe Clayton hasn't been the model husband."

"He hasn't been a husband, at all. *Or* a father."

Pete quickly stepped to the mare's side to glare at Carol over the animal's back. "Now wait just a damn minute. Clayton loves those kids."

She stopped brushing and rested her forearm along the mare's spine. "Yes, I think he does," she said, meeting his gaze levelly. "But the sad part is, he doesn't know how to express it."

"And you're a professional when it comes to dealing with relationships head-on, aren't you, Carol?" He knew the blow was low and well aimed. But he didn't care. She'd hurt him when she'd disappeared from his life, and the need for revenge was strong.

He watched her face pale, then she took a step back, dragging her hand from the horse's side. Turning away, she tossed the brush into the tack box. "Don't go there, Pete."

"Why not?" he asked, rounding the horse to confront her. "You don't seem to mind talking about other people's relationships, their feelings. Why can't you talk about your own?"

When she angled her head to look at him, the eyes that met his were emotionless. "Because where you're concerned, I don't have any."

Taking the mare's lead rope, she opened the gate and led the horse out into the alleyway. Pete caught up with her just outside the barn. He grabbed her arm and whipped her around to face him, his fingers digging into the flesh above her elbow. "Yes, you do," he said, his voice tight with suppressed fury. "You loved me once. I know you did."

"No," she said, trying to pull free. "I never loved you."

He grabbed her other arm and forced her to face him. The mare shied away from the scuffle, jerking the lead from Carol's hand, then trotted over to graze on the grass growing at the side of the barn.

"Yes, you did," he growled and gave Carol a shake, determined to make her admit it. "I tasted it every time I kissed you. Felt it every time you put your hands on me. I saw it in your eyes when we made love."

Panic filled her green eyes, and she frantically shook her head, denying his claim. "No. I didn't love you. I didn't."

He jerked her up hard against him. "Yes, you did." Then, as if even now he could prove it, he crushed his mouth over hers. He felt her resistance, tasted the denial on her tightly pressed lips...and was even more determined to make her remember what they'd once shared.

He swept his tongue along the seam of her lips and, when she kept them stubbornly pressed together, wondered if he'd been wrong. Maybe she didn't love him. Maybe she never had. But then he felt a shudder pass through her, and her lips parted beneath his on a low moan of surrender while her hands climbed up his chest to curl around his neck. He felt the dig of her short, blunt nails in his skin as she drew his face closer, the fullness of her breasts as she surged against him, the desperation of a long-suppressed need as she mated her tongue with his.

Carol. Oh, Carol. What happened to us? he cried silently.

Tightening his hold on her, he lifted, drawing her to her toes, and thrust his tongue between her parted lips, deepening the kiss. The early morning sun bored down on his back, and a rivulet of sweat trailed irritatingly down his spine. A memory pushed itself into his mind of another time when he'd held her just this way, the sun warm on his back. Drawing her down to a quilt spread beneath the shade of the old live oak tree that grew on the rise just above her house. Watching the dappled sunshine play over her bare breasts. Feeling the heat of her body burning beneath his. Tasting her. Filling her. The mindless pleasure of losing himself in her, making her his.

But she wasn't his. She'd cut him out of her life, refusing to see him and never returning his calls.

Remembering that, he pushed her from him, his chest heaving as he stared down into her flushed face. Her lids fluttered up until her gaze met his. He saw the passion that glazed her eyes, the brief flicker of disappointment that he'd ended the kiss...and he knew he was right. She did love him. Or, at the least, she wasn't as unaffected by him as she tried to pretend.

Slowly her hands slipped from around his neck, and she dropped them to her sides. She took a step back, then another, the heat in her eyes giving way to a cool indifference.

She swept her tongue lazily across her upper lip. "You still know how to kiss a woman, Pete. I'll give you that." Turning her back on him, she strode for the side of the barn where the mare grazed.

Two

"**W**ho's that man?"

Carol glanced down at Adam, her first student of the day, then followed the line of his gaze to where Pete was riding away from the barn, Clayton's cow dog trotting closely behind. The straw hat Pete wore was old, stained and pulled low over his forehead, shadowing his face. But she could tell by the way he sat in the saddle—shoulders square, spine as straight as an arrow—that he was still angry with her. Even the way his fingers curled around the lariat he held against his leg—knuckles white against his tanned skin and digging into his thigh—was an indication of his dark mood.

With a sigh she turned back to the mare she was saddling and pulled the cinch tight. "That's Pete Dugan."

"Is he a rodeo cowboy?" Adam asked, squinting up at her.

"Yes."

"Is he a roper like Clayton?"

Chuckling, Carol squatted down, putting herself eye level with Adam. At six, his heroes were all still cowboys. "No, he's a bronc rider."

His eyes, already magnified by the thick lenses of his glasses, grew even larger. "For real?"

Laughing, Carol tapped the brim of his cap, knocking it down over his eyes. "Yes, for real." She rose, drawing her hands to her hips. "Now, are you ready to ride this old bronc?" she asked, nodding toward the horse she'd just saddled.

Adam shoved up the cap and scowled at the mare who stood placidly at the arena fence. "Honey's not a bronc. She's just a horse."

Carol bent over and cupped her hands, offering Adam a boost up to the saddle. "That's what you think, buster. Honey may not buck now, but when she was younger, there wasn't a cowboy around who could ride her."

Adam planted a boot in her hands and swung a leg over the saddle as she hefted him up. "No foolin'?"

"No foolin'." She gathered the reins and passed them to him. "Warm her up, okay? Three laps at a walk. Two at a trot. And remember your posture. Head up, back straight, heels down."

"You think she can still buck?" Adam asked hopefully as he turned the mare for the arena gate.

Carol bit back a smile. "You never know," she

called after him. "Better keep a deep seat and a tight rein, just in case she takes a mind to unload you."

She laughed softly as she watched Adam grab for the saddle horn. Shaking her head, she turned and glanced back in the direction where she'd last seen Pete. He was still in sight and, judging by his posture, he was still angry.

With a sigh she stooped to pick up the tack box and set it alongside the fence and out of the way. She'd purposefully hurt Pete and made him angry with her. Not that she'd enjoyed doing so, or had even wanted to. She'd never wanted to hurt Pete. Not then, and not now. But she couldn't get involved with him again. Not when she'd spent the better part of two years trying to forget him.

I didn't come to see Clayton. I came to take care of the place while he goes chasing after Rena.

Remembering his explanation of his unexpected appearance at the barn earlier that morning, she stifled a groan of frustration. And how in the world was she supposed to forget him, if he was going to be staying right next door?

She would avoid him, she told herself as she swung the arena gate closed behind her. She'd conduct her lessons, feed her horses and make sure she stayed out of his way. And if they did happen to cross paths while she was at Clayton's ranch, she'd ignore him…or, at the very least, feign indifference. She could do that, she told herself. After all, she'd successfully managed to avoid him for two years, which was no small feat, considering she lived right next door to one of his best friends.

Saw you at the rodeo last night. Were you there to watch me ride?

Scowling, she squinted her eyes at Adam, who was still walking Honey around the arena, warming up the mare for their lesson.

Wasn't it just like Pete to assume that she'd gone to the rodeo just to watch him ride? She had, of course, but she would choke before she'd admit that to him. Oh, she'd known she was taking a chance by attending the rodeo, but she hadn't been able to resist the opportunity to watch him ride, to see him again. Not when she knew he was competing within driving distance of her home. Not when there wasn't a single day that passed that she didn't think of him, wonder about him, dream about him.

But she hadn't intended for him to ever know she was there. And he wouldn't have known, either, if that bronc he'd ridden hadn't chosen the spot right beneath her box seat to scrape Pete off his back. Everyone in the section of seats, her included, had run to the rail to see if he was hurt. But when he'd looked up, it was her face he'd focused on. And when she'd seen the surprise in his eyes, the recognition, she hadn't been able to look away.

She'd look away this time, though, she told herself as she watched Adam smooch Honey into a trot. And she'd stay away, too. Far away.

Pete slapped the coiled rope against the leather chaps that protected his legs from the thorny mesquite trees scattered around Clayton's ranch. "Get up there," he called to a calf that had begun to lag. Clayton's dog, a blue heeler named Dirt of all things, barked and raced over, nipping at the calf's rear hooves. The calf bawled and ducked back into the herd, pushing its way to the center.

Wiping the back of his hand across his dry mouth, Pete glanced toward the barn. He'd avoided the area all day, working his way down the list of chores Clayton had left, careful to choose tasks that kept him away from the house and the barn. But Clayton had indicated that a buyer was coming to pick up the calves the next morning, and Pete was left with no choice but to round them up and head them for the barn and the corral beside it.

As he drew closer, he could see that Carol's truck was still parked beside the building, but thankfully she was nowhere in sight. He'd monitored her movements throughout the day—but from a distance—watching cars arrive and kids spill out, ready for the horseback riding lessons Troy had told him she offered in Clayton's arena.

He pushed the calves on, hoping that he could pen them in the corral and skedaddle before she appeared again.

"Damn," he muttered in frustration when he saw the gate was closed. Wishing that he'd thought to open it before he'd left to gather the calves, he turned his horse, planning to make a wide arc around them, open the gate, then slip back up behind them and push them through.

Just as he started to touch his spurs to his horse's side, he caught a flash of yellow out of the corner of his eye, and saw Carol step from the barn, a feed bucket in hand. She glanced his way, immediately saw his problem, and hustled over to swing the gate wide. Frowning, he turned his horse back behind the herd. Dirt darted from one side of the small herd to the other, barking and urging the calves on. When the last calf slipped inside the corral, Carol swung the gate closed and latched it into place.

Pete mumbled a begrudging, "Thanks," and turned his horse for the barn. At the hitching rail, he reined his horse to a stop and dismounted. But as soon as his right boot hit the ground, taking his full weight, his knee buckled and he crumpled. Howling in pain, he wrapped his arms around his leg and rolled to his side, curling his body protectively around the injured knee.

He felt a tentative hand on his shoulder, then the warmth of Carol's body as she knelt behind him. "Pete? What's wrong?"

He heard the concern in her voice, but had to clamp his teeth together to fight back the dizziness, the pain. "My knee," he managed to grate out.

With her hand braced on his shoulder, she stretched across him and smoothed her other hand down his thigh, her touch so gentle it brought tears to his eyes. But in spite of her care not to hurt him, when her hand swept across his swollen knee, he couldn't suppress the moan that swelled up inside him. He released his hold on his knee and rolled to his back, flinging his arms wide. She quickly moved out of his way and stood, staring down at him, her eyes wide with horror. His chest heaving, he squeezed his eyes shut and clawed his fingers at the hard-packed dirt, searching for something to anchor himself to, something to grab a hold of to lift himself above the pain. Something to hide behind, so Carol wouldn't witness his weakness.

Knowing it was useless, he opened his eyes to find her still standing above him, her fingers pressed against trembling lips, tears glistening in her eyes.

Humiliated by his weakness, he tried to make light of it. "Gee, Carol," he said, trying to force a smile past the pain. "I didn't think you cared."

At the teasing remark, she yanked her hands to her sides and glared down at him. "We need to get you to the house," she snapped. "Can you walk?"

"Yeah." He set his jaw and hauled himself to a sitting position. "I think so." Keeping his movements slow and careful, he drew up his good leg until his boot was fitted tightly against his buttocks. Beads of sweat popped out on his forehead at the effort. Blowing out a long, shaky breath, he rested a minute, then stretched out a hand. "I might need some help."

She hesitated a moment, then thrust out her hand. He took it and wrapped his fingers tightly around hers.

"On the count of three," he instructed. "One...two...three!" He heaved and Carol pulled, and with a growl he rose from the ground. Not wanting to put any weight on his bad leg, he staggered, off balance, and Carol quickly slipped beneath his arm and braced herself against his right side, supporting him.

"Give me a minute," he gasped, sweat pouring down his face. He dipped his chin and closed his eyes, gulping in air. After a moment he lifted his head and looked across at the house. Five hundred feet stretched like a mile.

"Come on," she urged, obviously sensing his hesitancy. "You can do it." Wrapping her arm around his waist, she took a tentative step, then another, drawing him along with her.

By the time they reached the back door, sweat plastered Pete's shirt to his back and chest and dripped from his nose and chin. With a quick glance at his pale, pain-wrenched face, Carol opened the back door, braced her hip against it, then carefully guided him through the opening. Once inside, she pressed him on toward the master bedroom.

When they reached the side of the bed, Pete twisted around and fell across the tangled covers with a groan, slinging an arm over his eyes.

Carol immediately dropped to her knees and tugged off his boots, knowing that he would need to remove his jeans before his knee swelled any more. Setting the boots aside, she rose and reached for his belt buckle...but jerked her hands back as she realized the intimacy that would require. She stole a glance at him and was relieved to see that his arm still covered his eyes, and he was unaware of her hesitancy. Frowning, she slapped a hand against the side of his uninjured leg. "Come on, Pete. Drop your pants."

He lifted his arm to peer at her. "'Scuse me?"

She waved an impatient hand at him. "You haven't got anything that I haven't seen before, so drop 'em."

In spite of the pain, Pete managed a weak grin as

he reached for his belt buckle. "Maybe not anything different, but definitely more of it."

She rolled her eyes and grabbed the waist of his jeans. "Braggart," she muttered.

His grin broadened into a full-blown smile. "No brag, ma'am. Just fact." He lifted his hips as she carefully worked the denim down over them, then sucked in air through his teeth when her hand grazed his manhood. She froze at the contact, her gaze snapping to his.

Pete watched the color rise on her cheeks, the panic in her eyes...and remembered a time when such an intimacy would have darkened those green eyes with passion, not panic. "Don't worry," he said wryly. "My knee's hurtin' so bad, you couldn't get a rise out of me even if you worked at it."

Her cheeks flaming, she jerked the jeans down his legs, making him yelp as the rough denim scraped over his swollen knee.

She spun away, folding his pants over her arm. "I need to feed my horses," she said tersely, tossing the jeans over a chair. "Do you need anything before I leave?"

That she couldn't look at him, or wouldn't, irritated Pete. "A phone. I need to call Clayton and tell him to head home."

She whirled, her eyes wide. "But you can't! He hasn't had a chance to talk to Rena yet."

He scowled and shifted a pillow beneath his knee, gritting his teeth against the pain that even that slight movement caused him. "So what? You said yourself that he was wasting his time chasing after her."

At the reminder, she caught her lip between her

teeth and dropped her gaze, lifting a shoulder. "Yes, I did, but still…"

"Look, Carol," he said in frustration and grabbed for the sheet. "It isn't as if I *want* to call him home, but I can't take care of his ranch for him if I'm laid up in bed."

Slowly she lifted her gaze. "You could if I helped you."

He froze, his fingers fisted in the sheet. "Help me?"

"Yes," she said, and took a reluctant step closer. "You could tell me what needs doing, and I could do it. Just until the swelling goes down," she added quickly. "A couple of days off that knee, and you should be able to take over again."

Still scowling, Pete tried to whip the sheet over his propped-up leg, but it snagged on his toes and hung there.

Carol plucked the sheet free and pulled it up over him, letting it drop to settle at his waist. The ease with which she accomplished the task irritated him, but her reluctance to draw near him or touch him irritated him even more.

"We could do it, couldn't we, Pete?" she asked hopefully. "It would give Clayton the time he needs to work things out with Rena."

He stared at her, amazed, after what she'd said earlier, that she'd willingly to do anything to help Clayton win back his wife. "Well, yeah, but that's easy for me to say since I won't be doing anything but lying here in bed and giving orders."

"I don't mind the extra work. Really I don't."

"Are you sure?"

"Positive." She stooped to pick up his boots and set them out of the way, then headed for the door. "I'll feed my horses, then I'll come back and you can give me a list of chores for tomorrow."

"Will you hand me my pain pills before you go?" He pointed at his duffel bag. "They're in the side pocket."

She fetched his pills and a glass of water from the bathroom. Keeping a safe distance, she set both on the bedside table within his reach, then headed for the door. "I won't be gone long. About an hour or so."

"Check and see if there's water in the trough for those calves I penned. Oh, and Carol!" he called after her. "You might ought to throw down a couple of bales of hay for them."

Carol methodically worked her way through her chores at the barn, putting out hay and oats for her horses and filling their water buckets.

But her mind wasn't on her work.

It was centered on Pete.

How was she going to avoid him, when she'd have to see him every day in order to get a list of chores?

Frowning, she climbed the ladder to the loft. She wouldn't be able to avoid him. Not entirely. Not now. Not after she'd offered to help him take care of the ranch. She dragged a bale of hay to the loft doors that opened over the corral, her frown deepening.

"Dang fool," she muttered, cursing herself as she yanked a pair of wire cutters from her back pocket.

"Why couldn't you keep your mouth shut? Why did you have to offer to help him?" Slipping the tool between the thin wire wrapped tightly around the bale, she snapped the handles together, snipping the wire in two.

She hadn't made the offer to help Pete because of any latent feelings she had for him, she told herself as she tossed down squares of loosened hay into the corral below. She'd made the offer for Rena's sake. Rena was her friend and, despite what Carol had told Pete earlier that morning, she knew Rena wanted their marriage to work.

Sighing, she straightened and looked out over the land where the sun was dipping low in the western sky. Rena and Clayton had had a tough time of it, she reflected sadly. An unexpected pregnancy that had forced them into a marriage neither of them were prepared for. The birth of the twins. But in spite of the circumstances of their marriage, Carol knew that Rena loved Clayton. But did Clayton love Rena? Enough to put his family before his rodeo career? Enough to be the kind of husband and father that his family wanted and needed?

At the thought, she glanced toward the house, thinking of Pete and the similarities she saw in their past relationship. She envisioned him in the house as she'd left him, lying in Rena and Clayton's bed in nothing but his briefs. She knew that being around him again wasn't going to be easy. But she'd do what was necessary to give Rena and Clayton a chance to reconcile their differences.

Squaring her shoulders, she headed for the ladder and the house. She'd see that the ranch ran smoothly until Pete was back on his feet. And when he was...well, she would avoid him, just as she had planned to before.

At the back door she shucked off her dirty boots, then tiptoed across the kitchen and down the hall that led to the master bedroom, keeping her tread light in the event that Pete had drifted off to sleep. When she reached the open doorway, she glanced toward the bed, but found it empty.

"Pete?" she called softly, looking around. When she didn't hear a reply, she called a little louder, "Pete?" When he still didn't respond, she ran for the master bathroom. She found him there, lying in a crumpled heap on the floor.

"Oh, my God," she cried and dropped to her knees beside him. She placed a hand on his cheek and turned his face toward hers. A lump the size of a marble swelled from his left temple.

"Pete?" she whispered, choked by the fear that crowded her throat. When he didn't respond, she quickly rose to dampen a washcloth, then knelt beside him again. "Pete," she repeated frantically as she bathed his face. "Come on, Pete, talk to me."

His eyelashes fluttered, and she lifted the cloth, clutching it to her breasts, her breath locked tightly in her lungs as she watched his eyes blink open. His gaze met hers, and he squinted, slowly bringing her into focus.

"Carol?" He tried to sit up, but sank back to the floor with a groan.

"Did you faint?" she asked, leaning over him.

"I...I don't know," he said, his voice thready and weak.

"What were you doing out of bed?"

"Had to pee. I—" he groaned again and lifted a trembling hand to his forehead. "Took a pill. Made me groggy."

"You should've waited until I got back," she scolded, "so that I could have helped you."

"Don't need a woman to help me pee," he grumbled.

Frowning, she tossed the washcloth to the sink, then bent over to slip an arm beneath his shoulders. "We need to get you back to bed. Can you walk?"

"Y-yeah. I...I think so." He pressed an elbow against the floor and, with her help, levered himself to a sitting position. He sat there a moment, breathing hard, his shoulders stooped, his hands dangling limply between his knees.

"Are you okay?" she asked uneasily.

"Give me a minute." He inhaled deeply, then reached up to brace a wide hand on the edge of the sink. Holding his injured leg out in front of him, he hauled himself awkwardly to his feet. Carol followed, supporting him as best she could with an arm wrapped around his waist. He hopped a couple of steps, his lips pressed tightly together, avoiding putting weight on his right leg. His face was chalk-white, and sweat glistened on his forehead at the effort.

"Just take it slow," she instructed nervously. Holding on to him and taking as much of his weight as possible, she slowly guided him back to the bed.

He collapsed across it, rolling to his back and throwing an arm across his eyes. Carefully Carol placed the pillow beneath his knee again, then straightened, looking down at him. His face was pale, his jaw slack, his chest heaving with each drawn breath.

And she knew there was no way she could leave him on his own for the night.

"I'm staying."

"I can take care of myself," he grumbled. "I don't need a damn nursemaid."

"Tough. You've got one." She snatched the sheet up and over his legs. "I'll need to run over to my house and pick up a few things. You stay in bed until I get back. I won't be gone long."

She started to turn away, but stopped when he caught her hand from behind. She squeezed her eyes shut as the warmth of his fingers closed around hers. It would be so easy to let the years slip away. To climb into bed with him. To wrap her arms around him and just hold him. To forget that he wasn't the man for her.

Taking a deep breath, she forced open her eyes and slowly turned back around, careful to hide her emotions from him. "What?"

"Thanks, Carol."

She swallowed hard, fighting the desire to go to him, to brush the damp hair from his forehead and press her lips there. To tell him how much she'd missed him. How many times she'd needed him. Slowly she eased her fingers from his and backed away. From him. From temptation.

"N-no problem," she stammered, then whirled for the door.

* * *

Carol parked her truck alongside her house and sank back against the seat, her heart heavy, her nerves raw. But as she stared at the white frame house with its dark-green shutters and its window boxes brimming with a profusion of trailing geraniums and sweet alyssum, the sense of satisfaction and pride she always felt when she looked at her home slowly filled her. This is what was important to her, she told herself. This is what she wanted. A home. Stability. Something she'd never known growing up. Something she would have lost if she hadn't broken off the relationship with Pete two years ago.

Though she only leased the property, she hoped to own it someday. That and the land that surrounded it. Abandoned for over five years, the house had been in bad shape when she'd first leased it. But she'd accomplished a great deal in the three years she'd lived there. She'd scrubbed it from top to bottom and given it a fresh coat of paint, inside and out. She'd repaired the fencing and made the old barn useable again. She hoped to add an arena soon, so that she wouldn't have to use Clayton's for her horseback riding classes. When she did, she'd be able to increase the number of classes she offered. Maybe even hold a few clinics.

And someday she hoped to have a family to share her home with.

Unconsciously she rubbed her hand down her thigh, still able to feel the warmth of Pete's fingers on her palm. She'd told herself a million times over the past two years that she'd done the right thing in ending the relationship with him...but she'd never

been able to forget him. Not entirely. Not when a
part of him would be with her always as a reminder.

Her gaze strayed to the oak tree that stood like a
sentinel on the small rise behind her house. Tears
blurred her vision as she stared at the old tree with
its barrel-size trunk and its low-hanging limbs. So
many memories were tied to that tree. So many
heartaches.

Slowly she climbed from the truck and started
toward the tree, stopping along the way to gather a
fistful of wildflowers. When she reached the top of
the rise, she dropped to her knees beneath the spread
of the oak's comforting limbs and carefully laid the
flowers on the ground. Sinking back on her heels,
she dipped her chin to her chest and let the tears
she'd suppressed all day fall.

Fresh from a shower and dressed for bed, Carol
stood in the doorway, tray in hand, staring at Pete,
unable to take that first step into the room where he
slept. He lay just as she'd left him earlier that evening—flat on his back, his propped-up knee tenting
the sheet she'd draped over it. Earlier, when she'd
helped him back to bed after his fall, he'd flung an
arm across his eyes, as if to block out the last rays
of sunlight that had spilled through the bedroom
window…or to block out the pain. His other arm
lay across his abdomen, bunching the sheet low on
his waist.

A wistful smile trembled at her lips as she noticed
that his thumb was hooked in the waist of his briefs,
a habit of his when he slept that she had often teased
him about.

She eased across the room and set the tray on the bedside table, then turned to look down at him, unable to resist this unobserved opportunity to do so. Each feature of his face was so painfully familiar to her, so dear. The roman-shaped nose, the high slash of cheekbone, the faint scar—a parting gift from a bronc he'd ridden—that ran like a railroad track along his right jaw. She had to lace her fingers together to resist the temptation to reach out and touch him.

As she stared, he flinched, as if in pain, then twisted, moaning his frustration when the pillow propped beneath his leg prevented him from rolling to his side. Fearing he might hurt himself again, she placed a hand against his shoulder and gently pressed him back against the pillow, then smoothed her fingers across his brow. "You're okay," she whispered, drawing her palm to his cheek to soothe him. "Just lie still."

Though his eyes never opened, his hand came up to cover hers, his fingers curling around hers. She inhaled sharply as the rough calluses on his fingers and palm chafed against her own softer skin. She had only to close her eyes to remember the feel of those hands on her body, the passion they could excite, the needs they could awaken.

Weakened by the memories, she sank to the edge of the bed. She remained there, her gaze fixed on their joined hands, her eyes filled with tears, remembering, regretting, until his breathing evened out and the tension melted from his face. She remained there until shadows filled the room and the soup she'd prepared for him grew cold on the bedside table.

* * *

"Carol?"

She jerked awake at the sound of Pete's voice and raised her forehead from his chest to peer at him. She blinked twice in the darkness before her eyes adjusted enough to see that he was awake and looking at her. Realizing that she had used their still-joined hands as a pillow, she quickly sat up and slipped her fingers from his, hoping he hadn't noticed the intimate gesture. "I'm sorry," she murmured in embarrassment. "I...I must've fallen asleep."

He caught her hand, stopping her before she could fully rise. "No need to apologize."

Though she'd been holding his hand for several hours, at the renewed contact, electrical shocks shot up her arm. Flustered by them, she tore her gaze from his. "I...I made you soup," she stammered inanely, gesturing toward it, feeling as if she needed to explain her presence in his room.

"I'm not hungry." He tugged her closer. "Are you?"

"N-no. I ate earlier." She watched the moonlight dance over his face and tried to think of something else to say, anything to strip the air of intimacy that suddenly seemed to fill the shadowed room. "Does your knee still hurt?"

He snorted a laugh. "My knee always hurts. That's a given." He shifted, making more space on the bed beside him. "But it doesn't hurt as much as it did earlier." He nudged the pillow from beneath his injured knee and rolled to his side. Giving her hand another gentle tug, he drew her back down on the bed beside him. With his gaze on hers, he curled his arm, drawing their joined hands to his chest. "I appreciate you staying to take care of me."

She could only stare, eyes wide and unblinking, as the steady beat of his heart pulsed against the back of her hand. "You...you're welcome."

"I've missed you, Carol."

The huskily spoken words were so unexpected that she dropped her chin to her chest, unable to think of a thing to say in return.

He reached up and swept back the hair that had fallen to curtain her cheek. After tucking the strand behind her ear, he placed his fingertips against her cheek and forced her face back to his. "I'd like to think that you've missed me, too."

"Pete, please—"

"Shhh," he whispered, and pulled her down to lie beside him. When she tried to sit back up, he slipped an arm over her, holding her in place. "I'm not going to try anything," he said as he snuggled her closer against his chest, holding their joined hands against his heart. "I just want to hold you. Be close to you. That's all, I swear."

She held her breath as his eyes drifted shut and his forehead came to rest against hers on the pillow they shared. Slowly she let the breath shudder out of her. Every nerve in her body screamed with awareness of each part of his body that touched hers. His forehead, the callused fingers clasped around hers, the muscled thigh, the brush of a bare toe. The hand he'd splayed across her back continued its mindless stroking, slowly coaxing the tension from her.

How many times had she lain with him like this?

she wondered. His arm wrapped around her, her hand gripped against his chest while he slept? The comfort and satisfaction she'd always drawn from simply being held by him, safe in the strength of his embrace, slowly stole over her. Tears burned behind her eyes. She didn't want to find security and comfort here. Not with Pete. Not when she knew he could never truly provide those things for her.

"Pete?"

"Hmmm?"

She'd intended to tell him to let her up, that she didn't want to be held by him, but before she could, he drew back and looked at her, his sleepy brown eyes filled with an endearing blend of tenderness and contentment in the moonlight.

"What?" he asked softly.

She stared at him, feeling the pressure of the tears building, knowing that what she wanted to say to him was a lie. A part of her still wanted him, still yearned for him, and always would. Even as she tried to squeeze back the emotion that rose, he was releasing her hand to brush a thumb across her lashes, stealing the tears that had escaped before they could fall.

He pushed himself up to an elbow. "Why are you crying?" he asked softly.

"It's just that…" Unable to find the words to explain her feelings, she caught her lower lip between her teeth and turned her face away.

He placed a knuckle beneath her chin and forced her gaze back to his. "You're remembering, aren't you?" he asked gently. "You're remembering how good things were between us?"

She shook her head frantically, choked by tears. "N-no, I—"

Then his mouth was on hers, a butterfly kiss, soft and coaxing, offering comfort and understanding, and any argument she might have given was lost. The taste of him, the texture of his lips moving over hers. The tenderness with which he soothed her. The strength in the arms that held her close. Every movement, every touch, brought back a memory, a need that she'd locked away two years before. And when he swept his tongue across the seam of her lips, she was powerless to do anything less than open for him, inviting him in as freely as she had then.

He shifted, rolling her to her back, his mouth still molded to hers. Then, slowly, he drew his lips away to look down at her. "I've missed you, Carol," he whispered, his brown eyes dark, piercing her soul. "I've missed holding you and kissing you." He swept the ball of his thumb across her cheek and smiled wistfully, watching its slow movement. "And I've missed looking at you, talking to you, laughing with you." He shifted his gaze to hers, and his smile slowly faded, his brown eyes searching hers. "I want to make love with you, Carol. I want to hold you while I sleep tonight and wake up with you by my side in the morning. But I have to know that you want that, too."

She couldn't answer him. The emotion that clogged her throat wouldn't allow a single word to squeeze through.

His expression turned fierce, his eyes darkening. "You loved me, Carol. I know you did. And you still have feelings for me." He dipped his head over hers, nipped at her lower lip, then soothed the spot with his tongue. "You can deny it all you want," he whispered against her trembling lips, "but I can see it in your eyes when I look at you." He closed his hand around her breast, molding his fingers around its shape. "And I can feel the need burning inside you, just like it's burning in me." He dragged his mouth over her chin and down her neck. "You want me, Carol, as badly as I want you. Don't deny it." He blew, warming her breast with his breath, then closed his mouth over the soft cotton that covered it and drew her in.

She arched high on a sob and filled her hands with his hair. He suckled her through the thin fabric of her nightgown, alternately nipping and soothing, then closed his hand around the fullness of her breast and slowly pulled her from his mouth. He glanced up at her over his brows, while he rolled her aching nipple between his thumb and finger. "Tell me you don't want me," he whispered. "Tell me, and I'll stop. I swear."

Three

"Tell me, Carol," he said again. "Tell me to stop."

Tears leaked from the corners of her eyes. The words were there, knotted in her throat. She wanted to tell him to stop, knew that she should before she lost all ability to reason. But as she stared up into his face, a face that was so dear to her, so missed, and felt the weight of his hand on her breast, the heat of the passion it drew, she knew that telling him to stop was beyond her power. "No," she murmured on a broken sob. "Please." She fisted her fingers in his hair and drew his face back to hers. "Don't stop. Please don't stop. I want—"

His mouth closed over hers, stealing her words, and their breaths became one. Ragged, gasping. Their hearts pounded frantically in unison, a shared rhythm of need and long-suppressed passion as he pressed his chest against hers, as if desperate to get closer still.

And Carol knew that she was lost. She was adrift in a sea of need that only Pete could fulfill. She loved him. She always had. Always would. And, at the moment, it didn't matter that she knew a relationship with him was impossible, even potentially self-destructive. *Now* was what was important. This moment. These feelings. Being with him. Satisfying this yearning that burned inside her, this need that had smoldered for two long years.

He slowly stripped her of her robe and nightgown, each sweep of his hands over her flesh shooting the flames higher, burning away all rational thought, blinding her to everything but him.

He tore his mouth from hers and stared down at her, his eyes searing into hers, his chest heaving. "Slow," he said, and gulped, swallowing hard. "I want it slow." When she would have argued, demanded that he take her now, he pressed his fingers against her lips, silencing her. With painstaking slowness he slid his fingers over her jaw and down her neck until his palm rested over her heart. Lifting himself higher on an elbow, he looked down at his hand where it lay against her moon-kissed skin, and drew in a shuddering breath. "You're so soft," he murmured, then lifted his gaze to hers. "I'd forgotten how soft."

She looked at him through a flood of tears and reached to lay a hand against the stubble of beard that darkened his jaw. And she'd forgotten how tender he could be. How unbelievably romantic a lover. But before she could tell him so, he shifted his gaze again and swirled his fingers around a breast, cupping it within his palm and making her suck in a breath. He raked a thumb across her nipple, watched it bud, then dipped his head low and laved it with his tongue.

She arched, moaning, as hot, piercing arrows shot through her body and embedded themselves, quivering, low in her abdomen. Heat spread in a molten river to every extremity, leaving her aching for more of his touch.

And more is what he gave to her. He seemed intent on driving her mad, smoothing his hands over every inch of her body, warming her flesh to fever pitch, tasting and pleasuring her with his lips and tongue. He found her more sensitive spots and teased until she could barely draw a breath, until her nerves burned and leaped beneath her skin, until she was sure she would scream in frustration if he didn't fill her.

Then, when she was sure she was near death, he rose above her, his eyes dark with heat as they met hers. He drew in a ragged breath, his chest expanding. Pads of hardened muscle swelled beneath darkly tanned skin and glistened beneath a silvery sheen of perspiration in the soft moonlight. With his hands planted on either side of her, bearing most of his weight, he nudged her legs apart and created a nest for himself.

Then, slowly, oh, so slowly, he lowered himself over her. Her eyelids grew heavy, too heavy to hold up, and she closed them, whimpering pitifully. She felt the weight of his thighs as they met hers, then the added pressure of his groin as he sank against her. She gloried in the feel of every inch of him that covered her...but wanted more. So much more.

"Look at me, Carol," he whispered. "Open your eyes and look at me."

She shook her head, moaning. "No, please, Pete." Blindly she reached for him, wanting to draw him down to her, wanting, more than her next breath, for him to take her, to fill her, to satisfy this raging need.

"Look at me," he said again.

She closed her hands around his arms, feeling the hardened muscle, the skin slick with perspiration. "Pete, please," she begged. She dug her nails into the hardness, straining against his greater strength...yet he refused to succumb to her. Using every ounce of her own strength, she forced her eyes open to meet his gaze.

"Keep them open, Carol," he whispered, shifting again and aligning his body over hers. "I want to see you when I fill you. I want to see the pleasure I give you mirrored in your eyes."

She gasped as his sex met hers, her eyes widening...then moaned, digging her blunt nails into his flesh as he slipped inside.

"Don't close them, Carol. Look at me."

Though it took all her strength to do so, she kept her eyes open and riveted on his. In the dark-brown depths, she saw the passion, the promise of pleasure, the heat of a need as strong as her own.

The muscles in his arms quivered beneath her hands as he struggled to remain above her...then he began to move, slowly at first, drawing her with him,

each thrust of his body spinning her higher and
higher toward the satisfaction that remained stubbornly out of reach.

"Pete," she gasped. "Pete, please!"

"Come on, Carol," he grated through clenched
teeth. "Come with me."

He growled low in his throat, and thrust again,
deeply, driving her higher still. She arched against
him, sobbing out his name as pleasure spilled
through her in waves that rolled and rolled, threatening to drown her. Then his mouth was on hers,
stealing what was left of her breath, and the weight
of his body came down on hers, pressing her deeply
into the mattress. Groaning, he dove his hands
through her tangled hair, his fingertips scraping
against her scalp as he held her face centered beneath his.

"Carol," he murmured against her lips. "Oh,
Carol," he said again and sighed.

Then, to her surprise, he rolled to his back, taking
her with him, laughing, the sound of his laughter in
the dark room rich and deep and full of pleasure.
"Carol, Carol, Carol," he said, his laughter turning
to a groan as he hugged her tightly to him. "Damn,
I've missed you."

Instantly awake, Carol flipped open her eyes. She
blinked twice in the early morning light flickering
through the bedroom window, wondering what had
awakened her and found herself staring into Pete's
sleeping face. He lay opposite her, a lock of hair
drooping low on his forehead, a day's growth of
beard darkening his jaw.

Pete?

Disoriented, certain that she was dreaming, she glanced around the room and realized that she was in Rena and Clayton's bedroom, not her own. Gradually she became aware of the weight of the arm that draped her waist, the pressure of the knee sprawled possessively across hers, and turned to look at him again...and remembered.

She'd made love with him. Fallen asleep in his arms.

She felt the panic growing in her chest, as strong as the urge to reach out and brush the lock of hair from his forehead, and tried to sit up. But the arm at her waist tightened, holding her down.

"Don't move," he murmured, his voice husky with sleep. "I want to hold you."

Even as the panic spun tighter, she knew she wanted the same thing. But she couldn't remain there with him. She had to get up. Away from him. She had to think.

"Pete—"

Three short blasts from an air horn outside interrupted her, and she strained to peer over his shoulder and to the window beyond.

"Ignore them," he murmured, snuggling her closer against his chest. "They'll go away."

"Who'll go away?" she asked in dismay, snapping her gaze to his face and eyes that remained stubbornly closed.

"The guy who bought Clayton's calves," he murmured, nuzzling her neck.

She strained to look out the window again and saw an eighteen-wheeler pull up beside the corral in the distance, its chrome trim catching the sunlight and reflecting it back at her. As she watched, the driver reversed, angling the long trailer he pulled toward the loading chute. She struggled beneath the weight of Pete's arm. "Pete, let me up. I need to supervise the loading and collect the payment."

He opened his eyes slowly to look at her, and the heat in the brown depths caught her breath. She stilled as he pushed himself to an elbow, never once moving his gaze from hers as he looked down at her. Slowly she sank back down to the pillow.

"I'll buy the damn calves," he murmured as he drew his arm from around her to capture the breast that his movement had exposed. "Hell," he whispered huskily and dipped his face low to lave the nipple. "I'll pay Clayton double what they're worth, if you'll just stay in bed with me."

With his breath warming her breast, his tongue playing havoc with her ability to breathe, to think, Carol wavered uncertainly. "But, Pete," she argued weakly, "you promised Clayton you would—"

"Four times what they're worth," he promised. "Clayton can retire on the profit he'll make."

Though the offer was made rashly and in the heat of passion, she knew Pete could well afford to pay Clayton whatever price he demanded for his calves. He made a sizable income rodeoing, and another small fortune with his endorsements. Tempted, she wavered uncertainly.

The air horn blasted a second time, and she groaned and shoved his face away. "You've got more money than sense, Pete Dugan," she said as she rolled from beneath him.

Already feeling the loss, Pete watched her push from the bed. ''Maybe,'' he murmured absently as he watched her reach for her nightgown, enjoying the view of her heart-shaped rear, the long stretch of firm legs. A groan slipped from his lips as she turned to look at him. Standing with the sunlight behind her, the nightgown clutched at her breasts, she resembled a Grecian goddess with her flame of red hair, tousled from sleep, draping her shoulders and curling seductively over her breasts. The gown she held flowed from her tightly fisted hands like a waterfall, streaming down between her legs and hiding just enough of her femininity to make him grow hard.

Slowly he lifted his gaze to hers. ''Ten times what they're worth,'' he amended, his voice raw. ''Just stay with me.''

''How's it goin'?''

Pete tucked the phone receiver between his shoulder and ear and gingerly lifted his leg to prop it on the ottoman he'd positioned in front of the bedroom window. ''Everything's under control here,'' he lied, not wanting to worry Troy by telling him about his reinjured knee. ''How about you? How was the rodeo in New Mexico?''

''Yuma made his throw. I missed mine by a mile.''

Shaking his head in sympathy, Pete sank back in the overstuffed chair and looked out the window to the corral in the distance where Carol was supervising the loading of the calves. ''Don't worry, buddy,'' he said, wishing like hell he'd been able to convince her to stay in bed with him. "Your luck's bound to change before long."

Troy's sigh was heavy with defeat and matched the one swelling in Pete's chest as he looked longingly at Carol, thinking of what they could be doing right now if only he'd been able to persuade her to stay in bed with him.

"Yeah," Troy said wearily. "That's what I keep telling myself, too." He sighed again, then asked, "Have you heard from Clayton?"

"Nope. Have you?"

"No, but then I didn't expect to. Figured he'd call you if he had any news."

"He'll check in when he can. Right now I'm sure he's got his hands full, dealing with Rena."

Troy's snort was short and full of disgust. "That man needs to get his head screwed on straight, before he messes around and loses his wife and kids. Rena's a good woman. Better than Clayton deserves, I'm ashamed to say."

"Yeah, she's a good woman, all right," Pete replied thoughtfully, though his comment reflected more his opinion of the woman he was watching through the window, than Clayton's wife.

There was a long pause, then Troy asked hesitantly, "Have you seen Carol?"

A slow grin spread across Pete's face. He could almost see Troy shuffling his big feet and rubbing a hand across the back of his neck as he worked up the nerve to ask the question. Of the three men, Troy was the quietest, most tenderhearted, the least comfortable when it came to discussing female relationships…a trait which Clayton and Pete teased him about unmercifully.

"As a matter of fact," Pete said, curling his hand around the phone's base and propping it low on his abdomen, "I'm looking at her right now."

"She's there with you?"

At the shock he heard in Troy's voice, Pete tossed back his head and laughed. "No, not right now. She's out in the corral, supervising the loading of some calves Clayton sold."

"Oh." There was another long pause, then Troy cleared his throat, a sure sign that he had something on his mind, but was having difficulty spitting it out.

"Listen, Pete," he finally said. "I was wondering…"

"What?" Pete prodded when Troy hesitated again, though he was sure he knew what his friend wanted to know.

"Well, I, uh, I was wondering if you'd, uh, well, if you've had a chance to, well, to talk to her?"

"Yeah, I did."

"Really? So, how'd it go?"

"How did what go?" Pete asked, enjoying giving his friend a hard time.

"Hell," Troy said in frustration. "You know what I'm wantin' to know."

Pete laid his head against the chair's cushioned back and laughed long and hard. "Everything's fine," he said as he turned his gaze on the window again. "In fact, better than fine," he added, his smile warming when Carol stepped into view again.

"Well, I'll be," Troy murmured in disbelief.

"Did she say why she wouldn't return your calls before?"

"No. We haven't gotten around to talking about that yet. But we will," he added confidently.

"Hang on a sec, Pete."

Pete could hear Troy talking to someone in the background.

"Listen, Pete," Troy said when he came back on the line. "Yuma's ready to hit the road, so I need to let you go. We're headed for Colorado, but we'll be swinging back toward Texas in a couple of days. I'll check in with you then. In the meantime, call if you need me."

"Don't worry about a thing. I've got everything under control here."

There was a short pause, then Troy said, "Pete?"

"Yeah?"

Another pause, even longer this time, before Troy added, "Take care of yourself."

By the gruffness in his friend's voice, Pete knew that what Troy was telling him to do was to protect his heart.

"Don't worry about me," Pete assured him. "I can take care of myself. You just concentrate on wrestling those steers to the ground and winning yourself some prize money."

"Good lesson, Misty. Your skills are really improving."

"Does that mean I'm ready to ride Clipper?"

Carol laughed and gave Misty's ponytail an affectionate tug. "Not quite. But soon," she promised when she saw the child's face fall in disappointment.

Misty scuffed the toe of her boot against a clod of dirt in the arena. "How soon?" She pouted. "I'm tired of riding Honey. She's nothing but an old plodder."

"Shhhh," Carol said, lifting her hands to press them over the horse's ears. "You don't want Honey to hear you say that. You'll hurt her feelings."

Misty rolled her eyes. "Miss Carol, horses can't understand English."

"Sure they can." To prove it, Carol dropped the lead rope, then pulled off her cap and tossed it to the ground. She walked away a few steps, then turned and stretched out her hand. "Honey," she ordered firmly. "Bring me my hat."

While Misty watched skeptically, the horse dropped its head and bumped its nose against the cap. Misty's eyes widened when Honey scooped up the hat, catching it between her teeth, then walked over to Carol and nuzzled it into her outstretched hand.

"Wow!" Misty cried, her eyes now as big as silver dollars. "I didn't know Honey could do tricks."

"That's nothing. Watch this." Carol tugged the cap back over her head, then picked up the lead rope. Filling her hand with the horse's mane, she swung herself up onto the horse's bare back. "Now watch carefully," she instructed Misty.

Using her legs to guide the animal, Carol had Honey spin in a full circle, stop, then spin back in the opposite direction. When she was facing Misty again, Carol had the horse back three steps, then, using the tip of her boot, she prodded the back of Honey's right leg. While Misty watched, slack-jawed, the horse dropped down to one knee and bowed its head.

"How'd you do that?" Misty asked, lifting her gaze to stare at Carol, her eyes wide with awe.

Carol slid down from the horse's back and gave Honey an affectionate pat as the horse rose to stand on all four legs again. "Signals. You know how I'm always telling you to use your legs?" At the child's nod, she said, "Well, that's how I did it. To get her to spin to the right, I open up my right leg and press against her side with my left. When I want her to spin to the left, I do the opposite."

"How about the bow? How'd you get her to do that?"

Carol laughed and turned back to the horse. "That's our little secret, isn't it, Honey?" she said as she rubbed the horse's nose.

"No fair!" Misty cried, running to tug on Carol's arm. "I want to get her to bow, too."

"But I thought you didn't want to ride Honey anymore?" Carol said, looking down at the child in mock surprise.

"Yes I do! Will you teach me?"

Carol knelt down in front of Misty. "First, you have to learn the leg commands. When you can get Honey to spin like I did, then I'll teach you how to make her bow."

"Promise?"

Smiling, Carol tapped a finger against the tip of Misty's freckled nose. "Promise."

"Am I too early?"

Carol rose and waved to Madeline, Misty's

mother, who was standing at the arena gate. "Nope. Right on time."

"How did the lesson go today?" Madeline asked as she slipped inside and closed the gate behind her.

Carol glanced down at Misty and shot the child a conspiratorial wink. "Great. I think Misty's going to be a trick rider when she grows up."

"Yeah, you get to ride horses and be outside and stuff."

"Which reminds me," Madeline began, then frowned when a loud clanging sound interrupted her. "What in the world is that awful noise?" she asked, turning to look in the direction of the house.

When she heard Madeline gasp, Carol winced, drawing her shoulders to her ears. She knew what the sound was and, more, she knew who was making it.

Pete.

And she also knew what a prankster Pete was. But what she didn't know was what lengths he would go to in order to get her attention. And that's what worried her. Fearing the worst, she turned to follow Madeline's gaze. But the sight that greeted her was much worse than any she might have imagined. Pete was leaning out the bedroom window, bare-chested, beating the clanger against the iron triangle dinner bell she'd given him to use to signal her in case of an emergency.

"Who is *that*?"

The shock in Madeline's voice didn't surprise Carol. Not when the window revealed only the upper half of Pete's body, making him appear to be wearing nothing but a straw cowboy hat. Heat crawled up her neck as she murmured, "That's Pete Dugan. A friend of Clayton's," she added quickly. "They rodeo together."

"Oh, my," Madeline murmured, placing a hand at her throat. "I had no idea cowboys were so—" She darted a quick glance at her daughter who was looking up at her expectantly, then pressed her lips together and turned to look at Pete again. "S-so fit," she finished awkwardly.

Carol bit back a smile as she moved to stand beside Madeline. "Cowboys have to stay in shape, the same as any professional athlete." And Pete was definitely in good shape, she thought, holding back a lusty sigh as she watched the muscles in his chest and arms bulge as he continued to clang the triangle.

And he was a clown, too, a trait that had delighted her years before, but worried her now as she watched him toss aside the clanger and lean farther out the window.

"Help!" he wailed, waving his arms wildly. "I'm being held hostage! I need food! I'm starving! Help! Please, somebody help me!"

"Oh, no," Carol murmured and fitted a hand to her brow, covering her eyes, as she dropped her chin to her chest.

Madeline whirled, her eyes wide, to stare at Carol in shock. "He's being held hostage?"

Knowing an explanation was needed, Carol sighed and dropped her hand. "No," she said wearily. "He just can't walk."

Madeline turned slowly to look at Pete again. "He can't walk? How sad," she murmured sympathetically.

"It's not a permanent disability," Carol assured her dryly, glowering at Pete. "He injured his knee while bronc riding and has to stay off his feet for a couple of days." She lifted a shoulder. "I'm looking after him, and I guess this is his way of letting me know he's ready for his lunch."

Obviously enjoying the attention his performance was receiving, Pete turned in profile and struck a muscle man pose, sucking in his stomach and bending his arm to make his bicep bulge.

Fearing what he might do next, Carol cupped her hands to her mouth. "We're just finishing up," she yelled to him. "I'll be there in a minute."

Grinning, he blew a kiss and waved, then ducked back inside the house, closing the window behind him.

Embarrassed, Carol murmured, "Sorry. Pete is…well, he's just Pete," she finished helplessly, unable to come up with the words to define his outrageous personality.

Madeline turned away from the now-empty window with a sigh. "Oh, to be single again," she murmured, then laughed and patted Carol's arm. "Well, I guess we'd better get out of your hair," she said, then shot Carol a knowing wink, "so that you can prepare his lunch."

That Madeline would suspect she was doing more than just caring for Pete had heat flooding Carol's cheeks. "I'm only helping out," she rushed to explain. "Until he's back on his feet again."

"Umm-hmm." Madeline hummed doubtfully, then laughed again. "Are we still on for Friday?" she asked, changing the subject.

Carol groaned at the reminder. "Oh, Madeline, I'm sorry. With all that's been going on, I forgot all about it. And I was counting on Rena helping me, but she's in Oklahoma, visiting her parents."

"I'm only bringing five students, and I'll have my assistant with me," Madeline added hopefully. "Don't you think that between us we can handle that many?"

Frowning, Carol debated postponing the field trip to the ranch Madeline had scheduled for her students, but quickly decided against it. She couldn't disappoint those kids. Not when they so looked forward to the excursions.

Forcing a reassuring smile, she nodded. "Sure we can." She glanced down at Misty and reached to tug on the girl's ponytail, grinning. "Especially if Misty is willing to help, too."

"Pete Dugan, I could just shoot you!"

Pete sat up straighter in the chair, looking up at Carol as she dumped the snack tray that held his lunch unceremoniously onto his lap. "What makes you say that?" he asked innocently.

She straightened, drawing her fists to her hips to glare down at him. "Hanging out the window half-dressed. And in front of my student and her mother, no less. And saying you were being held hostage." She huffed a breath. "You should be ashamed of yourself."

He bit back a smile as he calmly picked up the tray and leaned to set it on the floor beside his chair. Glancing back up at her, he caught her hand and reared back, tugging her closer. "How do you know

I was half-dressed?" he asked, teasing her with a smile.

Determined not to be charmed by him, she tried to pull free. "Because I saw you, that's how."

He merely tightened his grip on her hand and widened his smile, pulling her closer. "Couldn't resist looking, huh?"

Realizing he was stronger than she and sure to win the tug-of-war, Carol gave up trying to escape and replied dryly, "With the ruckus you were creating, you were a little hard to miss."

Keeping his gaze on hers, Pete drew her hand to his chest and rubbed the back of it across its breadth. He smiled, pleased, when he felt her pulse jump in reaction. "Bet you could hardly wait for them to leave so you could come back inside and have your way with me again, huh?"

She snorted, then lifted her chin and gestured toward the tray he'd discarded. "I thought you were starving."

He tugged again, harder this time, and laughed when she lost her balance, yelping, and tumbled across his lap.

Pleased with the success of his slick maneuver, he smiled down at her. "I am," he said, and smoothed the ball of his thumb along her lower lip. "For another taste of you." Before she could reply, he dipped his head over hers and covered her mouth with his.

Though Carol was determined to hold on to her anger, when his mouth closed over hers and his tongue slipped between her parted lips, she felt the anger slipping away. "Pete," she murmured, trying to hold on to it, "please." She wedged her fingertips between their lips, forcing his face back so that she could look at him. "I'm serious," she lectured sternly. "You can't pull stunts like that in front of my students. What will they think?"

"That I'm crazy about you?" He smiled and nipped at one of the fingertips she held against his mouth, catching it between his teeth. "That I'd do anything to get you back in my bed?" He caught her hand in his and held her fingers against his lips. "If that's what they'd be thinking," he murmured against them, "then they'd be right." He drew her hand away and leaned to brush his mouth over hers. "I *am* crazy about you. I spent the whole damn morning plotting ways to get you back inside this house and into bed with me." His lips spread into a smile against hers. "Just be glad the dinner chime worked. My next plan was much more desperate."

Weakened by his tenderness, the seductive pull of his voice, his irresistible charm, Carol peered up at him, knowing she was nothing but putty in his hands. "How desperate?"

He shifted his gaze from her eyes and to her cheek, biting back a smile as he tucked a strand of hair behind her ear. "Nothing too desperate," he said with an indifferent lift of his shoulder. "Just a little lighter fluid, a couple of matches. Of course, Rena would probably have killed me for torching her drapes."

Carol's eyes widened in horror. "You'd have set fire to her drapes?"

Laughing, he shifted, settling her more comfortably across his lap. "If that's what it took to get you

back in here. But I didn't have to resort to arson,''
he reminded her, and slipped a hand underneath her
blouse, starting a fire of a different sort. ''You're
here now, and that was my goal.''

Four

Carol gasped, tensing when his hand closed over her breast, then melted, sighing as he gently kneaded it. "But I'm not in bed with you," she pointed out breathlessly. "You said that was your goal."

He dropped the foot of his good leg to the floor and braced a hand against the chair arm and started to rise. "Guess I'm going to need that lighter fluid, after all."

She yelped, clinging to him, sure that he was going to dump her on the floor. "No! Please! Sit!"

"You sure?"

"Yes," she said, laughing, hanging on to him. "I'm positive."

He settled back in the chair and smiled as he reached for the top button of her blouse and toyed with it. "Good, 'cause Rena's real fond of those drapes.'' He worked his fingers down the front of her blouse, releasing each button, then folded back the plackets of her blouse. She shivered deliciously as he swept his palm across her midriff, his gaze locked on his hand's slow movement over her skin. He cocked his head to look at her. "Ever made love in a chair?''

"N-no, I don't think so.''

"Me, neither.'' He slipped a finger inside the waist of her jeans and worked the snap free. "Mind being on top?''

The scrape of his fingers against her flesh sent shivers of anticipation skittering down her spine. "No,'' she whispered, gulping, unable to take her eyes off him.

"Good, 'cause I'm afraid my knee isn't up to the gymnastics my being on top would require.''

She lifted her hips at his urging, and he slipped her jeans and panties over them and down her legs. "Now,'' he said, tossing them aside. His voice grew husky as he smoothed his palm up her leg, "Let's get down to business.''

She sucked in a startled breath when he cupped her, then released it on a rush of air when he lowered his face over hers.

"Slow or fast?'' he murmured against her lips. "This one's your call.''

Even as he asked the question, he plunged his tongue into her mouth and a finger deep inside her and sent her soaring. "Fast,'' she gasped, clinging to him as the first wave crested, dragging her under. He reached for the top button of his jeans, but her fingers found it first as she shifted over him, placing a knee on either side of his hips.

"Help me, Pete," she moaned in frustration when the snap stubbornly refused to open beneath her fingers' fumbling.

Bracing a hand on her back to hold her steady, he quickly freed the button, then lifted his hips and, one-handed, worked his jeans down to gather them around his propped-up knees.

"Easy," he murmured when she took him in her hand, then he closed his eyes and dropped his head back against the cushion on a groan as her fingers slid down his length, guiding him to her. Bracing his hands against her hips, he held her still, reveling in the feel of the heat, the velvet softness surrounding him. "Damn, you feel good," he whispered. Opening his eyes, he met her gaze. "Ride me," he urged as he lifted his hips to meet hers. "Ride me as fast and as hard as you want."

With his eyes burning into hers, his sex filling her completely, she gulped nervously. She'd never experienced this wild aggressiveness before, this crazed need for satisfaction, to dominate…but discovered that it aroused her as much as it frightened her.

Drawing in a deep breath, she rested her hands against his broad chest and rose, trembling, above him…then sank on a guttural groan, only to rise again, throwing back her head and sobbing out his name as pleasure spilled through her. Each ebb and flow of their joined bodies sent the heat raging higher, the desperate need for more twisting tighter.

Every nerve in her body quivered, every muscle

burned as she raced blindly for fulfillment, for a release from the flames of desire that licked at her, threatening to consume her.

Her eyes burning into his, she dug her fingers into his flesh, silently demanding a release from him. Even as she did, she watched his eyes darken and smolder, felt the muscles in his chest tense beneath her tightly curled fists. The growl that swelled from deep inside him vibrated through her, freeing the animal that clawed furiously within her, and shot her high and over the edge. She arched hard, bowing her back, and screamed his name, the sound echoing in her mind, in her heart. With another growl, he clamped his hands around her hips and held her against him as he pumped his hot seed into her.

Weak, sated, she hung there a moment, suspended, her head thrown back, her breasts rising and falling with each breath…then sank weakly against his chest and wrapped her arms loosely around his neck. Never in her life had she felt so wild, so free, so sated.

Never more exposed.

Every emotion imaginable crowded her throat as she lay there exhausted, trembling, her eyes wide and unblinking as she stared at the wall behind them. Happiness. Joy. Fulfillment. A love so strong it was a knot of pain in her chest, struggling to burst free.

But doubt was there, too, shadowing the other emotions. She'd never displayed such wantonness, such aggression before. Not with Pete. Not with any man.

She waited for him to say something, to do something. When he remained still and eerily silent, she buried her face in the curve of his neck and fought back the tears, the humiliation. She remained there until her heart steadied, until her breathing evened out, until she was sure she had her emotions under control enough that she wouldn't cry when she spoke.

"P-Pete?" she said uncertainly.

"Hmmm?"

"Th-that was good, wasn't it?"

He turned his lips against her neck. "Better than good. The best."

She went limp with relief at his reassurance, then shivered and smiled when she felt his lips spread in a grin across her damp skin.

"I'd say you scored about a ninety," he said offhandedly, then nipped playfully at her earlobe. "Of course," he was quick to add, "that bronc you were riding earned you more than half of those points."

She smothered a laugh in the curve of his neck, then pushed slowly from his chest to sit back on his thighs. "Really?" she said, feigning surprise. She pressed a fingertip to the middle of his chest and slowly dragged it down his stomach. "I thought the bronc was rather slow coming out of the chute, and I was thinking about demanding a reride."

Groaning when her finger bumped against the damp spot where their bodies still joined, he caught her hips and drew her more firmly against his groin. "Well, we'll just have to see what we can do about getting you that reride," he murmured huskily.

Carol didn't want to keep smiling...but she couldn't seem to stop. She drove Clayton's ranch truck from pasture to pasture, stopping along the way to dump salt blocks from its bed for the cattle to lick. The work was backbreaking and the heat relentless beneath the Texas afternoon sun, but in spite of it all, she couldn't seem to quit smiling.

She wanted to hug herself or, at the very least, preen…and only just managed to keep herself from doing both. But she couldn't seem to keep herself from smiling. And she couldn't seem to stop thinking about Pete, either, who waited back at the house for her return.

And she'd intended to avoid him, she reminded herself, chuckling. A plan that had lasted less than twenty-four hours. But she should have known that she wouldn't be able to resist him. Not Pete. He was irresistible—handsome, tender, passionate. And he was such a clown, always able to draw a smile from her, no matter what her mood, a trait that had attracted her to him when she'd first met him three years before.

Then she'd been serious, intense, rarely finding anything to smile about, much less laugh about. A by-product of a dysfunctional childhood that she'd never been able to escape, she knew. She sighed, her smile fading at the reminder of her family. An alcoholic father, who could never hold a job longer than six months at a time. One whose wild mood swings kept the entire family on edge, never knowing if a comment from one of them would win a hug from him or a smack on the face. A mother who struggled to make ends meet when her husband drank away his paycheck, their only livelihood. One who lacked the courage or the skills to leave him when he would break his promise to her to give up alcohol and would disappear for weeks at a time on a wild binge.

It was no wonder that she'd fallen head over heels for Pete, she thought sadly. He was like a breath of fresh air, healing sunlight, after being locked away in a damp, dark cell for so many years. Pete was affectionate and warm and full of fun. With him she had always felt safe, secure, loved. She'd been happy, deliriously so.

But that was before she'd discovered that Pete lacked one quality that was of extreme importance to her. Roots...or more, a desire for them. A home wasn't important to him, nor was settling down with a family. He was content living out of his truck, chasing from one rodeo to the next, his permanent address a post office box where he collected his mail, his sole means of communication a cell phone he kept tucked in his shirt pocket.

Had he changed in the two years they'd been apart? she wondered uneasily, as the doubts returned to chisel away at her happiness. Was he finally ready to settle down in one spot and take on the responsibility of a wife, a family, a home?

With a sigh she closed the last gate behind her, knowing that she didn't have the answers to those questions. Not yet. And when she did have the answers, she wondered, would her heart break all over again?

The cell phone rang as she turned for the truck, and she broke into a run, her heart thumping wildly, knowing it had to be Pete calling her. Snatching the

phone from the seat, she pressed it to her ear, sure
that he was calling to tell her he'd fallen again and
hurt himself. "Pete? Are you all right?"

"No. I'm lonely."

She sagged with relief, then smiled softly at the
little-boy pout in his voice. "I've only been gone a
couple of hours," she reminded him.

"That's a couple of hours too long. Forget the
chores and come home. I need you."

Propping a hip against the side of the truck, she
hugged the phone to her ear, loving hearing the
sound of his voice, the need she heard there, as well.
"Why?"

"Because I'm lonely."

She sputtered a laugh. "Heavens! If you're
lonely, turn on the television."

"I can't hold a television."

Already climbing into the truck, she laughed.
"Yes, you can. Just put your arms around it and—"

"That's not funny."

She put the truck in gear, as anxious to return to
the ranch house as he was to have her there with
him. "I'm not trying to be funny. I'm offering you
alternatives."

"What are you doing?"

"Driving."

"What are you wearing?"

She choked on a laugh at the outrageousness of
the question. "The same thing I was wearing when
I left the house."

"That's too damn many clothes. Take something
off."

Her eyes went wide at the suggestion and she

whipped the steering wheel to avoid hitting a block of salt she'd thrown out earlier. "I certainly will not! What if someone sees me?"

"Who would see you? You're in the pasture, aren't you?"

"Well, yes," she replied hesitantly, glancing nervously about.

"Take off your blouse."

"Pete!"

"Come on, Carol," he wheedled. "Just the blouse."

"Why?"

"Because I'm lonely, and I need something to think about to take my mind off my loneliness."

She rolled her eyes. "Pete Dugan, you're crazy."

"No, I'm not. I told you, I'm lonely."

"And me taking off my blouse is going to rid you of your loneliness?"

"No, it'll drive me crazy thinking about you bouncing around in that truck wearing nothing but your jeans. But that's better than being lonely."

Carol huffed a breath, unable to believe she was even having this conversation. "This is insane. I'm hanging up the phone."

"No! Don't hang up."

"Yes, I am. You're talking crazy." Pulling the receiver from her ear, she punched the disconnect button, cutting off his desperate pleas. The phone rang again just as she set it down on the seat beside her. Groaning, she snatched it back to her ear. "What?" she snapped impatiently.

"Did you take your blouse off?"

"No, I didn't take my blouse off, and I'm not going to, either!"

"That's okay. I'll use my imagination."

She inhaled deeply, searching for patience. "Pete. Go take a nap."

"Can't."

"Why not?"

"If I go to sleep, I'll just dream about you, and that'll make me even lonelier."

In spite of herself, Carol found herself laughing again. "You're hopeless."

"I know."

There was a long pause, then he said quietly. "Carol?"

"Yes?"

"Do you miss me?"

She started to laugh at the ridiculousness of the question, then caught herself, realizing that she *did* miss him, which was absurd, since they'd been apart for less than three hours. "Sort of," she hedged, not wanting to reveal too much.

"I miss you, too." A heavy sigh passed through the air waves and settled around her heart. "Carol?"

"Yes, Pete?"

"How long before you're home?"

She glanced at the house in the distance, imagining him sitting in the chair in front of the bedroom window where she'd left him. "If you look out the window, you can judge that for yourself."

She laughed when she heard a scrambling sound, then sobered quickly when she heard him swear. "What's wrong?" she asked in concern.

"I stubbed my toe."

"Poor baby," she murmured sympathetically. "Do you want me to kiss it and make it better?"

"No, I want you to take off your blouse."

"Pete!"

"Come on. I'll take off my shirt, if it'll make you feel better."

"You're not wearing a shirt," she reminded him dryly.

"Okay, then, I'll take off my jeans."

"Don't you dare."

"Why not? There's nobody around to see me but you."

"Well, yeah, but someone could drop by unexpectedly."

"Who?"

"I don't know," she said in frustration, "but it *is* a possibility."

"A small one." There was a shuffling noise, then he said, "Hold on a second."

She held the phone to her ear, keeping an eye on the house that was growing closer by the second and the bedroom window where she knew he was waiting. She chuckled as she watched the window rise, then Pete poke his head through the opening. He disappeared, then reappeared, holding the phone to his ear.

"Carol? You still there?"

"Yes," she said, laughing. "I'm still here."

"I have a surprise for you."

"What?"

"You'll see."

He disappeared again, and she waited, watching and wondering what the surprise was.

"Have you ever been mooned?"

Her mouth dropped open. "Pete Dugan don't you dare— Oh, my heavens!" She slammed on the brakes and clapped a hand over her eyes. Just to make sure she had seen what she thought she'd seen, she made a slit with her fingers and peeked through.

Dropping her hand, she stared a full five seconds before she let her head fall back and burst out laughing. "Pete?" she said drawing the phone to her mouth again.

"Yeah?"

"You're crazy."

"Yeah, I know. Crazy about you."

Carol turned from the stove, her eyes widening when she saw Pete walking into the kitchen, fully dressed. "You're walking!" she cried in surprise.

He swelled his chest and rubbed his palms briskly over the front of his shirt. "Since I was two," he said proudly.

Rolling her eyes, she set the fork aside and reached for a dish towel to wipe her hands. "Funny," she replied dryly. "I meant you're walking *now*. Should you be?" she asked, her frown turning to one of concern as she crossed to him.

He settled his hands on her hips and drew her abdomen to his groin, then bent his head over hers and stole her breath with a kiss. "It's been two days, nurse," he murmured, nuzzling her nose with his. "Don't you think it's time?"

"Well, yeah, I guess," she said uncertainly, then pushed from him to frown down at his knee. "Does it hurt?"

"Not any more than usual."

She blew out an unsteady breath. "I don't know, Pete," she said uneasily, then glanced up at him. "Are you sure you aren't rushing things?"

He laughed and slung an arm around her shoulders and guided her back to the stove where bacon sizzled in an iron skillet. "You're just trying to find excuses to keep me in bed, so you can have your way with me."

Heat crawled up Carol's neck at his teasing, suspecting that he might be at least partially correct in his assumption. But she would never admit to that. Especially not to him.

She sniffed indignantly. "I am not," she said, and shrugged from beneath his arm. She picked up the fork to turn the bacon, then sucked in a startled breath when his arms came around her from behind and the length of his body pressed against her back.

"Are you sure?" he teased, rubbing against her suggestively.

She inhaled sharply, then slowly released the breath, as the level of his arousal became evident. The heat rising from the stove was nothing compared to that which flooded her body. Furious that he could reduce her so quickly to such a quivering state of need, she decided to get even.

"Not that I didn't give it some thought..." she began slowly, then turned and slipped her arms around his neck. Smiling seductively up at him, she rose to her toes and closed her mouth over his. She kissed him deeply, swirling her tongue inside his mouth and mating it with his. She tasted the surprise, felt the heat, the need rushing through him and, satisfied, she withdrew, slowly dragging her lips from his.

With a regretful sigh, she sank back to her heels and ran her tongue along her upper lip as she looked up at him from beneath thick lashes. Seeing the heat in his eyes, the almost desperate way in which he was looking at her, she dropped her arms from around his neck with another sigh. "But then I remembered what chores awaited me today," she said sadly, "and decided that wouldn't be wise." Pleased with herself and her performance, she picked up the fork again.

"Carol?"

"Hmmm?"

"My knee's beginning to hurt."

She bit back a smile as she lifted the last strip of bacon from the skillet and transferred it to a plate. "Really?"

"Yeah. It's throbbing something awful."

"Gee," she said sympathetically, and turned to brush past him. "That's too bad. But are you sure that throbbing isn't occurring a little higher on your anatomy?"

"Carol?"

At the huskiness in his voice, the almost desperate way in which he said her name, she had to swallow back a laugh. "Yes?"

"I never knew you could be so cruel."

"Cruel?" she repeated innocently as she leaned to set the plate of bacon on the table.

She heard him groan, then whisper, "Oh, Lord. Don't do that again. Please."

She turned to peer at him, her confusion sincere this time. "Do what?"

"Bend over," he said, and swallowed hard, his Adam's apple bobbing convulsively as he shifted his gaze to hers. "Seeing you like that brings out the animal in me. All I can think about is making love with you."

Her pulse kicked, sending her blood racing as a mental picture of what he described formed in her own mind. She watched him reach for his belt buckle, and she widened her eyes, then narrowed them on him. "Pete," she warned, backing away, "we've got chores to do." He started toward her, tugging his shirttail from his jeans. She caught a glimpse—just a quick one—of the patch of dark hair that swirled around his navel and narrowed to a vee that disappeared behind the waist of his jeans.

Her mouth suddenly dry, she wet her lips, unable to tear her gaze away from the sight. "There's work waiting for us," she reminded him, and thrust out a hand to stave off an advance she feared she was powerless to resist. "We—" She squealed and turned to run when he grabbed for her, but he jerked her around and slammed her against his chest, his arms clamping like a vise around her. As she looked up at him, his mouth came down on hers, forcing her head back, his lips hard and bruising, demanding a response from her.

The heat was already there, banked low and smoldering. It leaped high at his insistent urging. She moaned, surrendering, and lifted her arms to fill her hands with his hair.

The world shrank to that spot in the kitchen. Time

stopped, freezing them in that moment of animal-like passion, that clawing desire. Carol wasn't sure how much time passed before she realized that the arms that had vised her before held her more loosely now; that the hands that had dug into her back, forcing her against him, were now gently kneading; that the lips that had crushed and bruised, were butter soft as they swept tenderly across hers.

"Carol?" he murmured.

"Hmmm?" she hummed weakly.

"Think the chores could wait awhile?"

She chuckled, the sound muffled by the lips still pressed against hers. "Probably."

The fingers that massaged his knee were tender, soothing, the body pressed snuggly against his back a comfort Pete hadn't experienced in a long, long time. He sighed his contentment in the darkness and closed his eyes, letting Carol's fingers work their magic on his stiff and aching knee.

"How'd you get this scar?" she asked softly, her fingertips tracing the ribbon of puffy flesh.

"Bronc riding."

She snorted softly, the breath blowing warm against his spine. "I figured that. But how?"

He yawned and fisted the pillow, bunching it beneath his cheek. "Being stupid. More than normal," he added wryly.

"What did you do?"

"Climbed on a bronc while I was drunk."

She pushed herself to one elbow to look down at him, her eyes wide in horror. "You didn't!"

"Yep, I did." Smiling softly, he rolled to his back

to look up at her. Moonlight illuminated her face, making her skin appear translucent, much like an angel's. But then he'd always thought Carol was angel material. "But I had a good excuse."

She huffed a breath, then firmed her lips as she fussed with the covers, straightening them over his chest. "No excuse is good enough to justify climbing on a bronc when you've been drinking."

"I hadn't *been* drinking. I *was* drinking, and, at the time, drunk as a skunk and feeling no pain."

A vision of her father slipped into Carol's mind, and she firmly shoved it aside. Pete Dugan was *not* like her father. At least not in that sense. Pete was *not* an alcoholic. In fact, she couldn't remember ever seeing him take a drink. "I didn't know you drank," she offered hesitantly.

"I don't usually, but that night I had me a reason."

"And what was that?"

He lifted a hand to cup her cheek. "My girl had just dumped me."

She felt the heat crawl up her neck as she remembered the occasion to which he referred. A phone call from Pete; the cool indifference with which she'd responded to all his questions; her refusal to meet him when he invited her to join him at the next rodeo; the end of the conversation when she'd suggested that he not call her anymore.

"That's no reason," she murmured, trying to avoid his gaze.

But Pete put pressure on the hand he held at her cheek, forcing her face back to his. "Yeah, it was. At least it was for me." He dropped his hand and rested it on his chest, but continued to peer up at her. "Got me a bottle of Jack Daniel's and tried to drown my sorrows." He chuckled ruefully. "But what I ended up doing was busting my knee and landing myself in the hospital."

"You shouldn't have gotten on that bronc, if you were drunk."

"That's what Clayton and Troy tried to tell me, but I wouldn't listen. Thought I was Superman or at least Wild Bill Cody." He sighed, remembering that night, that ride. "The whiskey slowed down my reflexes, made me sluggish. Came out of the chute, missed marking the bronc, and everything just seemed to go downhill from there. I'd put too much resin on my glove, hadn't worked it in well enough before the ride, and when the bronc threw me, I hung up. That horse was bucking like crazy, jerking me along at his side like a rag doll. I was trying my best to stay on my feet, but when I finally managed to work my hand free, that old horse spun, knocking me down to the ground beneath him."

He shook his head slowly, his eyes wide and unblinking as he stared up at the ceiling, remembering that night...the pain in his arm as he'd hung on while trying to work his hand free from the rigging, the whoosh of air when the horse spun into him, knocking the breath from him and slamming him to the ground. The hooves flying and churning above him and around him, grazing the side of his head, his arm, then the weight of one coming down on his knee. The pain that shot up his thigh like a blowtorch, blinding him. The dizziness. The darkness.

And, finally, waking up in an ambulance and hearing the sirens screaming.

Slowly becoming aware of the silence that filled the room, Pete turned to look at Carol and found her staring at him, her eyes liquid with guilt.

"Hey," he said softly, and rolled to his side, drawing her into his arms. "It wasn't your fault. It was mine. I was the one who climbed on that bronc."

He felt the shudder move through her, then the warmth of her breath as she turned her face into his neck. "I never meant to hurt you, Pete," she whispered tearfully. "I swear I never meant to hurt you."

Five

___

As hard as he tried, Pete couldn't seem to remove the guilt Carol had assumed when he'd told her how he'd received the scar on his knee. Though she tried to hide it, he could see the guilt in her eyes every time he glanced her way and caught her watching him sadly. He even sensed it in her touch, in the way she would smooth a hand over the scar, her fingers light, trembling as if trying to erase it.

And he didn't want her to feel guilty. He didn't blame her for the injury. Being stomped by that horse was his own damned fault and a chance he took every time he climbed on a bronc, drunk or not.

Wanting to strip her of the guilt, but not sure how he could achieve that, he strode for the arena where she was giving a private lesson to a towheaded boy who was wearing glasses thicker than a soda bottle.

He stood at the fence, silently watching, his presence unnoticed by the two inside.

"Fork 'em over, Adam," he heard her say firmly as she held out her hand. "You're not ready for spurs, yet."

Grumbling, the boy plopped down on the ground and unbuckled the spurs attached to his boot heels. "But I want to make Honey run."

"Patience, Adam," he heard Carol say wearily as she accepted the first spur. "You've got to walk before you can crawl. I won't allow you to wear spurs or use a quirt, until I'm sure you can control Honey."

"But this is so boring," the boy complained as he planted a boot in Carol's cupped hands and swung a leg over the saddle as she hefted him up. "Walking around and around in a dumb circle. I want to make her run, see how fast she can go."

Pete bit back a grin. He remembered that kind of impatience. The desire for speed, when slow work was required first to develop the skills, the confidence needed to handle a more spirited horse.

"Trust me," he heard Carol reply. "She can run. What concerns me is what would happen to you if she did."

Still smiling, Pete glanced at the horse, and the smile slowly melted off his face. Twister? No, it couldn't be, he told himself, even as he noted the dappled spots on her rump, the distinctive brand on her right foreleg.

He'd won his first National Championship on

Twister's back, a horse who, at that time, was still ranked as one of the best bucking horses in the country, despite her age. She'd been retired two years later and put out to pasture. Having a soft spot for the horse who had helped him win his first championship, Pete had tried to buy her, but the stock producer had adamantly refused every offer he'd made. That was four years ago.

And now Carol owned Twister. A fact that seemed more than a little ironic to Pete.

His hand shaking a bit, he opened the gate and stepped inside the arena, closing it behind him. His gaze riveted on the animal he started across the arena toward Carol.

"You have Twister," he murmured, still staring at the horse in disbelief.

She glanced up at him, then away, her cheeks flaming beneath the shade of the cap she wore, her body tensing defensively. "Yes, I do."

"Why?" he asked, not even trying to disguise his surprise.

She lifted a shoulder, frowning. "I needed more riding stock for my school and Twister was available."

"Available?" he repeated in disbelief. "I tried a hundred or more times over the years to talk Jacob into selling me that horse, and he refused. How'd you manage to get him to sell her to you?"

She tugged her cap lower over her brow, hiding her eyes from him, then gave her shoulder another jerk. "I don't know. I guess my timing was right."

A smile slowly begin to spread across Pete's face, one that originated deep inside his chest and warmed him all the way to his toes. Carol had bought Twister—the one horse he'd always wanted to own and the one Carol had known meant the world to him, since he'd never kept his affection for the horse a secret from her or anyone else. Though he couldn't imagine what lengths she'd gone to to purchase the horse, the fact that she had did something to Pete's heart. She may have cut him out of her life, but she'd never forgotten him. Her buying the horse proved that.

He slung an arm around her shoulders. "Honey?" he teased, hugging her against his side. "Why'd you change her name to Honey, when Twister fit her to a T?"

Obviously embarrassed, she tried to shrug free. "I don't know," she grumbled.

"Yeah, you do." He caught her arms, forcing her to face him. "It's because that's what I called her. My little Honey. My moneymaker. She was my jump into the big time, the catalyst that cemented my rodeo career."

Though she tried hard not to, Carol couldn't prevent the smile that tugged at her lips. She ducked her head and scuffed the toe of her boot into the dirt between them. "You always were crazy about that horse."

Laughing, he drew her beneath his arm and to his side as he turned to look at Honey again. "Yeah," he said with a sigh. He gave Carol a hard squeeze. "But not nearly as crazy as I am about you." He looked down at her but frowned when he saw her eyes widen in alarm. Then she was moving.

"Adam!" she screamed, racing across the arena. "Don't you dare!"

Pete started after her, quickly determining the cause for her panic. Adam was jerking on the reins and digging his heels into the horse's sides, trying to urge Honey into a faster gait. The horse's ears flattened, her eyes wide and darting, as she struggled to decipher the confusing signals she was receiving from her rider.

When the horse bolted, breaking into a run, Pete ducked behind Carol, hoping to cut the horse off before it managed to unseat its rider. Running alongside the horse, he grabbed the reins and managed to get an arm around Adam's waist and pull the boy from the saddle. Dropping the boy to the ground, he struggled to pull the horse to a stop. Once he had, Honey pranced away from him, her eyes wild, her head high. "Whoa, there, girl," he murmured soothingly. "You're okay."

"Adam! Are you all right?" he heard Carol cry from behind him as he slowly brought the horse under control.

"Yeah," the boy sniffed. "I just wanted to see if I could make her run."

Pete turned to see Carol gather the boy into her arms and hug him tight. Just as quickly she set him down and pushed him to arm's length, her mouth firm as she shook a stern finger in his face. "Adam Warner, don't you *ever* disobey me again, do you understand? You could have been hurt."

"I didn't mean to," he mumbled, sniffing. He cut a quick glance at Pete who was leading the now calm horse back to where the two stood. "I was just trying to get her to run,'' he said miserably, ducking his head in shame.

Holding the reins against his thigh, Pete squatted down eye level with the boy. "But you confused her," he told him, keeping his voice gentle but firm. "With you kicking and pulling on the reins at the same time, Honey didn't know what you wanted from her." He dipped his chin, angling his head to peer up at the boy's down-turned face. "And you hurt her, too. Did you realize that?"

Adam's chin came up, his eyes wide beneath his thick glasses, his face pale. Frantically he shook his head. "I didn't mean to hurt her. I didn't. I would never hurt Honey."

"But you did," Pete said, pressing his hand against his thigh as he stood again. "Let me show you something," he said, and turned to Honey. He placed his fingers against the shank holding the bit in Honey's mouth and gently pulled back on the reins. "See what happens to the bit when you pull back?" he asked, demonstrating. "See how it pulls the bit against her lips, forcing them up? If you pull too hard, or jerk the reins, that hurts a horse."

He turned to look down at Adam. "Put your finger in your mouth, like this," he instructed, opening his own mouth and placing the length of his index finger across the opening. "That's right," he said as Adam mimicked his movements. He moved closer to the boy. "Now feel the difference when I put some pressure on your finger, the same as Honey feels when you pull on her reins." He curled his finger and pushed the knuckle gently but firmly against the side of the boy's finger, and watched as

Adam flinched away from the pressure, his eyes widening in dismay.

"See?" Pete said and dropped his hand, satisfied he'd proved his point. "Only Honey felt that and a whole lot more when you were jerking on the reins. Plus," he added, "you were kicking her, telling her to run, the whole time you were pulling back and signaling her to stop." He glanced at Honey and shook his head sadly as he reached up to rub the horse between the eyes. "Poor girl didn't know what to do, so she panicked."

"I—I'm sorry," Adam murmured, his voice thick with tears. "I didn't mean to hurt her. I'd never hurt Honey on purpose."

"I know you wouldn't," Pete said, and smiled sympathetically as he hunkered down to Adam's level again. "The good news is that horses are forgiving. But you have to remember," he warned, "every movement you make on a horse's back is a signal, whether you mean them to be or not. Understand?"

Adam bobbed his head, his eyes still wide. "Yessir. I understand."

Pete smiled then and reached out to ruffle Adam's hair. "Good," he said, and stood. "Now how about climbing on this horse's back again, just to prove to Honey that there are no hard feelings?"

Adam swallowed hard as he looked up at the horse, the fear and reluctance obvious in his eyes. "She won't try to run away again with me, will she?"

"That depends on you," Pete said gently. He tucked the reins beneath his arm and made a cup of his hands, offering Adam a lift up on the horse's back. "Just keep your fingers light on the reins and your signals consistent," he reminded Adam as he boosted him up into the saddle. He passed the boy the reins, then gave him an encouraging pat on the knee. "You'll do just fine, cowboy," he said with a wink. "Just fine."

Nervously Adam gathered the reins in his hands and turned his face forward, locking his gaze between the horse's ears. "Walk, Honey," he said, his voice shaking a little as he gave the command.

Pete folded his arms across his chest and reared back, grinning. "You're doing great," he called after him. "Now ask her to trot."

He saw the boy's shoulders rise in a deeply drawn breath, then the reluctance in his voice as he ordered the horse to trot. Honey responded to the command and stepped into a slow, smooth trot around the arena.

Pete watched, his grin widening.

Carol moved to stand beside Pete, her gaze riveted on her student and his progress around the arena. "Thanks," she murmured.

Glancing down, Pete saw that she was still trembling, a result of the close call. Smiling, he draped an arm around her shoulders and drew her against his side. "Thinking of offering me a job?"

She snorted and dug her elbow into his ribs. "Yeah, right."

"No, really," he said, and turned his gaze back to Adam. "I think I might be cut out for this kind of work."

She sputtered a laugh, then sighed, leaning into him. "And give up rodeoing? I doubt that."

Pete watched Adam rein the horse around and head back toward them. "Might," he said, and bit back a grin. "Depends on what kind of inducement you're willing to offer me."

"Inducement?" she repeated, glancing up at him.

"Yeah, you know. Salary. Room and board." He lifted a shoulder. "Of course, if board were to include a spot in your bed, I'd probably find that particular inducement a bit hard to turn down."

Carol laughed again, her laughter drawn as much by the smile on Adam's face as Pete's outrageous teasing. "I'll give it some thought," she replied dryly as she stepped from beneath his arm. "That was much better, Adam," she called out, walking to meet the boy. "Your signals were much more clear, and you kept her under control. Good job."

Adam's expression turned hopeful, if a little hesitant. "Think I could run her now?"

"Adam!" she cried in dismay.

"You want to run her?" Pete asked, stepping up beside Carol. "Think you can handle that kind of speed? Honey's quick, I can attest to that from my own personal experience."

"You've ridden Honey?" Adam asked in surprise.

"Yep. Sure have. In fact," Pete added, tipping his belt buckle up for Adam to see, "Honey helped me win this."

Adam's eyes rounded as he stared at the huge silver buckle trimmed in gold, and the World Champion Bronc Rider emblazoned across its front. "Wow!"

"Of course, that was several years ago and before someone changed her name from Twister to Honey," he said, glancing back over his shoulder to shoot Carol a wink.

"Twister!" Adam repeated, obviously awed by the visions the name invoked.

"Yep. Twister. She could twist faster and buck harder than any other horse on the circuit."

"No kiddin?"

"No kiddin'," Pete said with a decisive nod of his head. "She and I met up a few times before she helped me win the championship, though. Dumped me in the dirt more than once, I'm ashamed to say." He dragged a finger along his jaw. "See that scar?" he asked, angling his head so that Adam could see the scar that ran like a railroad track along the line of his jaw.

Adam leaned down, squinting through the thick glasses. "Yeah. I see it."

"Got that one from her rear hoof. Clipped me with it after tossing me on the seat of my pants."

"Honey did that?" Carol asked, moving to peer up at Pete in surprise.

"Sure as heck did. You have to understand that horses, tame or not, are still wild animals," he said, turning his attention back to Adam. "Unpredictable, at best. Every cowboy who climbs on a bronc's back knows that and has a healthy respect for it. He also knows he's taking a chance of injuring himself every time he competes." He dropped his gaze to Carol's, seeing this as the perfect opportunity to erase some of the guilt she carried. "And the cowboy blames no one, when he *does* get hurt. Not even the horse," he said, and smiled as he turned his gaze back to Adam.

"How many times have you been bucked off?" the boy asked breathlessly, his face flushed with excitement.

Pete snorted a laugh. "Too many to count," he said wryly, then puckered his mouth thoughtfully as he pulled at his chin. "You still wanting to give old Honey a run?"

Adam caught his lower lip between his teeth. "Yeah. I...I think so."

"You know, I've been hankerin' to give her another go ever since I saw y'all out here in the arena. How 'bout if I ride with you? Just to give you the feel? It'll give me a chance to test my skills with her again."

Adam cut his gaze to Carol, his look imploring. "Could we, Miss Carol?"

Pete wasn't fooling her. She knew he was offering Adam a chance for speed, even though it was with a safety net of sorts attached to the gift. She was well aware, too, of the gift he'd just given to her by telling Adam the story behind his scar...a release from the guilt she'd felt since learning how Pete had injured his knee.

Her heart full to near bursting, she laid a hand on Pete's arm and squeezed, then shifted her gaze to Adam. "I guess so," she said reluctantly. "But just this once, understand?"

"Yes, ma'am," Adam said, grinning.

Pete grabbed ahold of the saddle horn and swung

himself up behind Adam. "Let 'er rip, cowboy," he said, grinning.

Cautiously Adam loosened his hands on the reins and gave Honey a light tap with his heels. "Giddy-up, Honey," he said, then groaned his frustration when the horse stepped off at a slow walk.

"Giddy-up?" Pete repeated, his voice thick with disdain. "That's greenhorn talk, boy. You gotta let the horse *know* what you're wantin' it to do. Now hang on to your britches, cowboy, 'cause we're fixin' to take us a ride." With that, Pete goosed Honey in the flanks, and the horse took off at a run.

Carol heard Adam's gasp, saw his eyes go wide as the horse's quick leap propelled him back against Pete's chest. She would have worried about him falling off, but she also saw Pete's arm go around his waist, holding him firmly in the saddle in front of him, as he joined his own wide hand with the boy's smaller one on the reins.

Sighing, she turned a slow circle, watching them, her heart growing softer by the minute as the two raced Honey around the arena. If asked later, she knew she'd be hard-pressed to determine whose smile was bigger…Adam's or Pete's.

When things were going too well, Pete had a tendency to start worrying, expecting any second for the wind to change direction and a streak of bad luck to blow in to cause him havoc for a while. And that's what he found himself doing as he went about his chores in the barn, cleaning out stalls. Waiting. Watching. Expecting any moment for something to happen to rob him of his current good mood.

He figured he'd inherited the tendency from Troy, who had to be the world's biggest worry wart. He chuckled as he thought of his buddy. He missed Troy. And Clayton, too, for that matter. Though different as night and day from him in personality, the two men were his best friends. He would give either one of them the shirt off his back, if he thought they needed it, and they'd do the same for him, he knew.

He glanced across the barn at Carol, who was sitting on a bale of hay, cleaning her tack. A frown plowed her brow as she slowly rubbed saddle soap into the leather of the saddle perched on a rack in front of her.

He stopped raking, drawing the pitchfork against his chest and propping his chin on top of its handle. Something was bothering her, he knew, which was the basis for his own growing worries. He would catch her like this every once in a while, a frown knitting her forehead, a sadness in her eyes that seemed to come out of nowhere. But when he would ask her about it, she'd force a smile and say nothing was wrong, she was just thinking.

The hell of it was he was sure he knew what was on her mind. She was thinking about him leaving. After over a week on the ranch, he was as aware as she was that his time there was drawing to an end. Even if Clayton wasn't ready to come home, Pete knew that he couldn't afford to stay on much longer. Each day he spent off the circuit cost him a chance at earning prize money. And he needed the wins to ensure a trip to Las Vegas, come December, where the National Finals were held.

He sighed and grabbed up the pitchfork again,

scooping it into the sawdust scattered across the stall's floor. Asking her what was troubling her would be a waste of his time, he knew. And even if he were able to wrangle the truth from her, what would he do, what would he say?

He wouldn't make her any promises that he knew he wouldn't keep. And Pete Dugan wasn't a stayin' kind of man.

Carol lay in the bed, staring up at the ceiling, wondering why she felt so blue, so edgy when Pete was lying right beside her, sleeping, his arm draped comfortingly in the curve of her waist.

She couldn't remember ever being happier, more content. Staying with Pete at Rena and Clayton's house, sleeping with him, laughing with him and making love with him. But even as she thought of those things, a sense of foreboding slowly crept over her, and doubts began to crowd her mind.

She had been too happy, too content, she decided, blatantly ignoring what she knew was coming. Anytime now Clayton would return and Pete would leave, his services no longer needed at the ranch.

And when he left, what would happen to her? she wondered, her heart beginning to beat as if something wild was trapped in her chest. What would happen to the relationship they'd begun to rebuild? Would it be like before, when he would call her in the middle of the night, high after a win? When she would see him only in short snatches of time as he passed through Austin on his way to another rodeo or another public appearance for one of his corporate sponsors? Would her life revert back to living by a telephone, praying for it to ring, desperate for even that tenuous connection with him? To sitting in front of a television set for hours, holding her breath during that measly eight seconds when he was on the screen making his ride, needing desperately to see him, to connect with him, to prove to herself that the man she loved really existed and wasn't just some dream, a figment of her imagination?

Feeling the tears building, the fear cinching tightly around her chest, she rolled from beneath the weight of his arm and away from him. Shakily she stood with her back to the bed as the panic continued to build. Then, giving in to it, she bowed her head and covered her face with her hands.

She couldn't live like that again, she told herself, feeling the hysteria building. She wouldn't. She wouldn't sacrifice her dreams, her own needs, for his.

"Carol?"

She jerked up her head at the sound of his voice and dragged her hands to her mouth, smothering the sob that rose.

She heard the bed squeak behind her as he stretched across it, then the warmth of his hand on her back.

"Carol, what's wrong?"

She swallowed hard, forcing back the tears, the emotion. The fear. Slowly she dropped her hands. "N-nothing."

There was a rustle of movement behind her as he swung his legs over the side of the bed. Then his hands were at her waist and he was drawing her back between his legs and down to his lap. "You're trembling," he said softly as he wrapped his arms around her and laid his cheek next to hers. "Did you have a bad dream?"

She squeezed her eyes shut, not wanting to feel the warmth of his body seeping into hers or to find comfort in the darkness from his voice. "I...I—yes," she finally said, deciding that was as good an excuse as any to hide behind.

"Which one of the three *S*s was it?" he asked, nuzzling his nose at her neck.

Startled by the question, she turned her head slightly to look at him. "What?"

"The three *S*s. Snakes, spiders and sharks. Which one of the three *S*s were you dreaming about?"

"The three *S*s?" she repeated in bewilderment. "Where in the world did you hear that term?"

He shrugged and lay back, pulling her down to the bed to lie beside him. "Those are my biggest fears and the ones that cause me the worst nightmares." He shuddered and rolled to his side to face her. "Big hairy spiders crawling all over me." He curled his hand into a claw and walked his fingers over her stomach, demonstrating. "Man-eating sharks. Their mouths open, teeth bared, circling me and waiting for the chance to snap off my legs." He shivered again and wrapped his arm around her, drawing her close. "Scares the peewaddlydoodle out of me, just thinking about it."

She knew he was just jabbering to distract her, to take her mind off whatever worried her, and the thought that he would do that drew tears to her eyes.

"And then there's that third *S*," he said, and slipped a hand in the space between them to toy with the thin satin ribbon tied just above her breasts. "Snakes," he said in a low whisper, and glanced nervously around, as if in voicing the word out loud, he might have conjured them. "They're the worst. Long and slithering. Millions of 'em." He glanced up at her. "Have you ever seen any of the Indiana Jones movies?"

In the moonlight that spilled over his face, she saw the concern in his eyes, the uncertainty, and knew, at that moment, that she hadn't fooled him. He knew what was wrong with her, he knew that she was already thinking about him leaving. "Y-yes," she said, feeling the tears building again.

He frowned and turned his attention back to the ribbon again. "Old Indy was scared of 'em, too. Terrified, in fact. And wasn't too proud to admit his fear. Have to admire a man who can do that."

Her heart breaking, she laid a hand against his cheek and smoothed a thumb beneath his eye. "And what are you afraid of, Pete Dugan?" she asked softly. "What is it that terrifies you?"

She watched his fingers still on the satin ribbon, saw his lips firm, felt his jaw tense beneath her palm…and knew that this was the moment of reckoning. The moment when her heart would either fill with joy or be broken again.

She hadn't expected him to respond, or, if he did, she'd thought he'd make some joke, carefully avoiding giving a serious answer to her question. She was shocked when instead he replied in a voice so low she had to strain to hear it. "I don't know that I can put it into words."

"Try," she urged gently, knowing they both

needed for him to do so, in order to determine if they could resolve the issues that stood between them.

"I'm afraid of losing you again." He looked up at her then, and she saw the tears that glistened in his eyes. "I know I am," he said, his voice husky with them. "And it scares the hell out of me."

"Why would you lose me, Pete?" she asked, dreading his answer, but needing to hear it. "I'm not going anywhere. I'm right here. I've always been here."

She watched the anger build on his face, the frustration, and was shocked by it. Then he pushed off the bed, and paced away, dragging a hand through his hair.

He whirled furiously to face her, his hair spiked, his eyes wild. "Then why did you leave me before? Why did you cut me out of your life without a word of explanation?"

Suddenly Carol felt as if a spotlight had been turned on the bed, totally exposing her, every secret of her past hovering at the light's edges, lurking in the shadows, dangerously close to being exposed, as well.

Slowly she sat up and dipped her chin, watching as she gathered between her fingers the ribbons that Pete had untied. "Because I wanted permanence. Roots. Stability." She wound the ribbons as she spoke, pulling them into a loose bow, then stood. She lifted her chin defiantly when she met his accusing gaze. "Remember the last time we talked?" she asked him. "You were in Wyoming. I was here at home, miserable, lonely, missing you. And I was scared, too. Scared that that was the only kind of relationship we would ever have, and one exactly like the one that was tearing Rena and Clayton's marriage apart. You in one state, me in another, and nothing but phone calls to ease the loneliness. I needed you that night, Pete. I wanted to tell you that—'' She clamped her lips together, before she could say more, before she said something she would regret.

She inhaled deeply, then forced herself to go on. ''I asked you questions, leading questions, trying to get a commitment from you, trying to find out what your intentions were.'' She choked on a laugh, rough with tears. ''And I found out,'' she said bitterly. ''Oh, boy, did I find out.''

''Carol, I never meant to hurt you.''

''Hurt me?'' she repeated furiously. ''You broke my heart! You ripped it out of my chest with your glib answers, your fancy two-stepping evasions, and tore it to smithereens. But you won't again,'' she warned him darkly. ''I won't let you.'' Certain that he would if she remained, she snatched her clothes from the back of the chair and ran for the door.

''Carol! Where are you going?''

She stopped, her chest heaving, her heart breaking, and braced a hand against the jamb but refused to turn and look at him. ''H-home,'' she whispered. ''Home,'' she repeated more firmly, then used the jamb to propel herself through the doorway.

Six

The phone was ringing when Carol stepped into her dark house, but she ignored it, knowing it was Pete calling, and proceeded on to her bedroom, not bothering to turn on a light. The ringing stopped after a moment, and she almost wept with relief as the blessed silence settled around her.

Then it began again, its insistent ringing winding her nerves tighter and tighter until she was sure she would snap. Finally she snatched up the receiver from the bedside table. "I don't want to talk to you," she cried angrily, then on a sob said, "*please* don't call me again."

She slammed down the receiver without giving Pete a chance to say a word, then sank down on the bed and covered her face with her hands. The tears that soaked her palms were hot, the shudders that racked her slender shoulders strong enough to snap bone. She cried until she was sure she didn't have any more tears to cry, then wept even more, the grief ripe, the sadness, the regret weighing like an anvil on her chest.

The following morning Carol furiously cleaned house, certain that she'd emptied herself of tears the night before. But they continued to leak from her eyes, dampening her cheeks.

Furious that she couldn't seem to stop, she dragged a hand beneath her eyes as she pushed open the back door with her hip and leaned to shake out the hooked kitchen rug. Dust billowed in a cloud around her, gathering in her throat and stinging her already-swollen eyes. She turned her face away, coughing, and squeezed her eyes shut, trying to avoid as much of the irritating dust as possible.

When she was satisfied that she'd removed all of the dirt from the rug, she turned and tossed it across the porch railing for an airing. Then, drawn by the warm sunshine, she stepped out onto the porch, letting the screen door swing closed behind her. She folded her arms across her breasts and turned her face up to the sky. Inhaling deeply, she closed her eyes and let the sun's rays dry her cheeks, promising herself that when she opened her eyes, she wouldn't cry anymore. When she did open them, she stared at the clouds skittering across the blue canopy overhead and waited, testing. When they remained clear and dry, she heaved a sigh of relief and turned back for the house.

And that's when she saw them. Tucked up against

the side of the door, their petals drooping, their colors fading. Bluebonnets, soft-pink rose mallows, Indian blankets with their vibrant reds and splashes of bright yellow, black-eyed Susans. Wildflowers in a profusion of color, bunched together in a crude bouquet and tied with a worn strip of leather.

She whirled to look behind her, her heart thumping wildly against her ribs, expecting to find him standing there, fearing she would. But her yard was empty. Nothing but the wind rustling through the leaves of the old oak tree disturbed the peaceful solitude.

Slowly she turned back around and sank to one knee, gathering the wilted bouquet within her trembling hands. Standing, she drew the flowers to her nose. Tears streamed down her cheeks and fell to glitter like diamonds on the drooping blooms.

Oh, Pete, she cried silently. Please don't do this. Don't hurt me any more.

Pete sat on the porch steps, his shoulders hunched, his forearms braced on his thighs as he methodically shredded a toothpick between his fingers. In the distance he could hear the cattle calling, the sound low and lonesome in the dark night.

Lonesome.

He sighed and tossed the toothpick aside, propping his back against the trunk-size cedar porch post, and looked out across the dark, shadowed land. Lonesome was a mood he was beginning to feel with more and more regularity, but never stronger than the one that currently held him in its grip.

He missed Carol. Wanted to see her, talk to her.

Hold her. But she didn't want to see him. Hell, she wouldn't even answer her phone, and he'd called her at least a hundred times off and on during the day, after dropping off the bouquet of wildflowers just after dawn. And he knew she was home, because he'd even driven by earlier that evening to see if her truck was parked at her house.

But he hadn't been able to work up the nerve to turn into her drive, knock on her front door. Not when she wouldn't even talk to him on the phone.

He knew he'd hurt her, had seen the hurt in her eyes, heard it in her voice when she'd stormed from Clayton's bedroom the night before. But he'd been so stunned when she'd told him why she'd left him two years before that he hadn't been able to do anything but watch her go.

Not that he didn't remember the phone conversation she'd referred to, the one where she'd quizzed him, in a roundabout way, feeling him out about marriage, children and settling down with a family. Even now, when he thought about their conversation, he could taste the acid her questions had drawn, feel the panic burning a hole deep in his belly.

Pete Dugan might be a lot of things…but he was no family man. The mere thought of taking on the responsibility of a wife and family filled him with a fear that shook him to his toes and had him wanting to run as fast as he could in the opposite direction.

With a sigh of disgust he pushed himself off the steps. No, Pete Dugan wasn't a family man. He was a coward. A yellow-bellied, sniveling coward, just like his old man.

He stopped, bracing his hands on his hips, and

turned his face up to the sky, staring at the moon that hung like a gold-plated sickle embedded in a freshly plowed field of midnight blue. But he wouldn't hurt her, he told himself. She deserved more than what he had to offer her…which was a big, fat, disappointing nothing.

Carol heard the rumble of the school bus and stepped from the open barn door, lifting a hand to shade her eyes as she watched its slow approach. Her eyes widened in dismay when she saw the number of heads that bobbed behind the bus's windows as it neared.

Five! Madeline had said five, she cried silently as she did a rough count. But there had to be at least ten kids in that bus, if not more! She watched the bus's approach in growing alarm, wondering how on earth she could possibly deal with ten kids alone, with no one but Margaret and her assistant to help her. She'd have to cancel, she told herself firmly, at least the horseback riding part of the tour. There was no way that she could handle ten children with no one experienced around horses other than herself.

The bus ground to a halt, yellow lights flashing, and the doors folded back. Misty skipped down the steps, smiling broadly. "Hi, Miss Carol!"

Carol forced a smile in return, giving Misty a quick, if distracted, hug when the child raced over and wrapped her arms around her legs. "How many students did your mother bring?" Carol asked as she strained to see through the bus's windows.

"Twelve, I think. Mrs. Bowman was sick today, so Mom had to bring her class, too."

"Twelve?" Carol repeated weakly.

"Yep. Can I ride Clipper?"

"Not today, Misty. I'm going to need your help on the ground." Plus the help of a small army, she thought in growing dread as she watched the electric ramp lower. The first wheelchair appeared, and Carol forced her smile up another notch. "Hey, Jimmy!" she called, hurrying over to unbuckle the straps that held the boy's chair to the ramp. "How're you doing, cowboy?"

Jimmy looked up, his head wobbling on a neck not strong enough to hold it erect, his fingers curled into claws against the chair's arms. He offered her a lopsided grin. "Ride horse, 'kay?"

The excitement in his eyes stripped Carol of her plan to cancel the horseback riding part of the tour. She couldn't disappoint them, she told herself. If it took her all day and half the night, she would personally lead all twelve of the handicapped kids around the arena, making sure that they each had an opportunity to ride a horse.

"Sure, champ," she said, and leaned to give him a hug. "Anything you want."

Pete caught the corner of the towel wrapped around his neck and wiped the remaining shaving cream from his face as he stepped from the steam-filled bathroom. He squatted down beside his duffel bag and dug through it, looking for a clean shirt. When he didn't find one he stood, frowning, then with a shrug, crossed to Clayton's closet and opened the door. Choosing a freshly laundered chambray shirt from the rack, he stripped it from the hanger, then swung a foot behind him as he turned and gave the door a nudge, closing it.

He was going to call Clayton as soon as he was dressed, he promised himself as he crossed to the window. And he would tell his friend that he was either going to have to come home, or find someone else to look after his ranch, because Pete was leaving. He couldn't stay any longer. Not now. Being around Carol, having to see her, would be more painful than he thought either one of them could stand.

He would do this one last thing for her, he promised himself. He would get out of her life, and this time he'd stay out.

Sighing, he braced his hands on the windowsill and leaned to peer through the glass, his unbuttoned shirt falling open to expose his bare chest. He stared unseeing a moment, then slowly focused, his eyes going wide.

"What in the Sam Hill…" He leaned closer to the glass, watching Carol push a wheelchair toward the arena, her red hair tied up in a ponytail and gleaming in the bright sunlight. He quickly shifted his gaze to the four horses saddled and tied along the fence.

"Surely not," he muttered under his breath, then turned his gaze back to the bus. His eyes went wide again. He counted five, no, six wheelchairs, holding children of different sizes and gender, already aligned alongside the bus. Two women fussed around them, straightening caps and hats, setting brakes.

Inside the bus he could see another six faces peering through the windows, obviously waiting their turn to be unloaded. A little girl, no bigger than the chair she pushed, grunted and strained as she shoved one of the wheelchairs and its occupant toward the arena. The boy in the chair was laughing and clapping his hands, obviously excited about the upcoming ride.

Pete straightened, swallowing hard, unable to take his eyes off the scene unfolding in front of him. Three adults, one kid no bigger than a minute and twelve handicapped kids. And Carol was going to give them all rides? He slapped a hand against the back of his neck as he turned away and rubbed, thinking, debating, vacillating, then muttered a curse and started for the door, buttoning up his shirt.

"Hey, there, kids! Y'all going on a trail ride?"

Carol froze at the sound of Pete's voice, then forced her hands to finish unbuckling the safety belt that held Jimmy in the chair.

Not now, Pete, she prayed silently. *Please not now.*

"Well, hello!" Carol heard Madeline gush. "You must be Pete."

Carol snorted a laugh, remembering the woman's preoccupation with Pete's physique earlier that week when he had been hanging from the window half-dressed. Unable to resist, she glanced in the direction of the bus in time to see Pete sweep off his hat and bow low to Madeline.

"Yes, ma'am, in the flesh. And what would your name be?"

"Madeline. Madeline Moore. I saw you the other

day in the window, when you were clanging that awful bell. You didn't have a shirt on, and you were—"

The memory must have been too much for her, because she turned a brilliant shade of red and grabbed wildly at her assistant as the woman walked by. "This is Gracie," she said breathlessly, yanking the woman to her side. "Say hello to Pete, Gracie."

Gracie, bless her heart, was a spinster, pushing fifty, nearsighted and had never had a date in her life. But she stared at Pete with the same slack-jawed fascination as would any fifteen-year-old with raging hormones when Pete took her hand and squeezed it between his own.

"Pleased to meet you, Miss Gracie," he said, and charmed her with one of his most winning smiles. "And what's your name, sweetheart?" he asked, squatting down and putting himself eye level with Adrienne, a thirteen-year-old girl afflicted with cerebral palsy from birth.

"That's Adrienne," Misty said, skipping up to join them. "She can't talk."

"Really?" Pete turned his smile on the girl in the chair. "I'll bet if you could, you'd tell me what a handsome man I am, now, wouldn't you, Adrienne?" He laughed good-naturedly, then popped a quick kiss on her cheek and rose, patting her on the shoulder as he slipped behind her chair. "Now, which one of these wild broncs are you wanting to ride, cowgirl?" he asked as he pushed her chair toward the arena.

Scowling, Carol unclipped the catheter bag from Jimmy's chair and clipped it to her belt, trying her best to ignore Pete as he drew near. "Okay, Jimmy. Are you ready?"

The boy bobbed his head and clapped his hands, the childlike reaction a strong contrast to the soft stubble of beard that shadowed his jaw. A child locked inside a man's body, Pete thought sadly. And how in the world did Carol think she was going to load him on a horse? He pulled the brake on Adrienne's chair and leaned to whisper, "I'll be right back, cowgirl," then headed toward Carol.

He quickly unfastened the bag from Carol's belt and nudged her aside as he clipped it to his own. While she sputtered indignantly, he braced his hands on his knees and stooped down, putting his face directly in front of the boy's. "How old are you, Jimmy?"

"Eighteen," the boy lisped, ducking his head shyly.

"An old man," Pete said and grinned. "Bet you have to beat all the girls off with a stick, don't you?"

"Pete, really," Carol began, but he held out a hand, staving her off. With a huff of breath, she folded her arms across her breasts and stepped back.

"Ever ridden a horse before?" Pete asked Jimmy. "Uh-uh."

"Well, you're in for a treat, then, cowboy." He worked a hand behind the boy's back. "Wrap your arms around my neck, okay, partner?"

"'Kay," Jimmy replied and lifted his arms.

"Hang on tight now," Pete instructed as he pulled the boy up, then slipped a hand beneath his knees and lifted him up high on his chest.

"Wouldn't want to drop you in that pile of fresh manure."

Jimmy giggled and buried his face in the curve of Pete's neck.

Carol hurried to catch up. "What do you think you're doing?" she whispered furiously.

"Giving Jimmy a ride. That is why he's here, right?"

"Yes, but I don't need your help."

Pete ignored her and kept walking. "Didn't say you did."

"But you don't know what you're doing. These kids need special help."

Pete stopped beside a horse and shifted Jimmy in his arms. "I know what I'm doing. Step around on the other side," he said with a jerk of his chin, indicating where he wanted Carol to stand, "and brace him as I set him up in the saddle."

Muttering under her breath, she marched to the opposite side of the horse and reached up to support Jimmy while Pete ran straps over the boy's thighs and around to his back, drawing them up over his shoulders, then down across the boy's chest before securing them to the saddle horn.

"How's that?" Pete asked, squinting up at the boy. "Feel tight enough?"

Jimmy bobbed his head, grinning. "Ride horsey, ride horsey," he chanted in a singsong voice.

"Here," Pete said and passed the lead rope to Carol. "You take Jimmy while I get Adrienne in the saddle."

Her mouth hanging open, Carol stared after Pete as he strode away.

* * *

Carol couldn't believe it. If she hadn't witnessed it with her own eyes, she *wouldn't* have believed it. Pete, a professional cowboy, who rode some of the rankest roughstock rodeo producers could offer, who made a sizable income on the side smiling for cameras while wearing tight-fitting jeans provided by his corporate sponsor, jogging alongside a fat-bellied mare, holding a handicapped child up in the saddle. Laughing with the children, joking with them, wiping drool from their mouths, dropping his cowboy hat over their heads and making them smile.

No. She wouldn't have believed it.

And she certainly wouldn't have believed that it would have softened her heart toward him.

But it had.

And because it had, she wanted to get away from him. Far away. Yet he remained stubbornly at her side as she stood in the drive, waving to the children as the bus pulled away.

As she stood, watching dust rise in a cloud behind the bus's rear wheels, she knew, at the very least, she owed Pete a thank-you. Without his help she would never have been able to give the children the horseback rides they so looked forward to. But even the thought of saying thank you to him left a bitter taste in her mouth.

Pursing her lips, she turned away. "Thanks," she muttered resentfully and headed for the arena to unsaddle the horses.

To her dismay and growing frustration, Pete fell into step beside her. "Glad I could help. Cute kids. Do they come here often?"

She reached the fence and the line of horses tied there. Frowning, she lifted a stirrup and hooked it over the saddle horn. "Once a month," she replied tersely.

"Really?"

She heard the surprise in his voice, but chose to ignore both it and his question as she loosened the cinch, hoping he would take the hint and leave.

He didn't.

Instead, he slipped into the space between the horse she was unsaddling and the one tied next to it and flipped up the saddle's fender. "How much do they pay you?"

She jerked the cinch strap free, her frustration nearly choking her. "Nothing," she snapped. "I do it for the kids."

He turned his head to peer at her over his shoulder. "That's a mighty fine thing to do, Carol," he said after a moment, then turned around and went back to unsaddling Honey. "A mighty fine thing, indeed."

She frowned at his back as she stripped the saddle from Clipper's back. "You don't have to help me. I can handle things now."

He lifted the saddle from Honey and turned. "I'm sure you can. But I'm here, and I'm helping." Leaving her with no argument to offer, he headed for the barn and the tack room.

Grudgingly Carol followed. She heaved the saddle she carried onto the wall rack, then turned, gesturing for Pete to place the one he held on the rack beside it. She stepped back out of the way and folded her arms across her breasts. In spite of her determination to remain aloof, she found herself saying, "It didn't seem to bother you to handle all the kids' medical paraphernalia."

He lifted a shoulder. "I'm used to it."

She frowned as she watched him flip the saddle blanket across the top of the saddle to dry. "You are?"

"Yep." He turned, dusting off his hands, to look at her. "At one time or another my mother was hooked up to just about every device known to man. IVs, catheters, braces, monitors." He lifted a shoulder again. "You get used to it."

"Your mother?" she asked, unable to stem her curiosity. She'd never heard Pete speak about his parents before.

"Yep." He stalked past her and headed for the door.

Carol followed, her mind whirling with a million questions. "Was she ill?"

"Invalid. She was in a car wreck when I was a kid." He laid a hand on a horse's rump and ducked between it and the next one in line waiting to be unsaddled. He hooked the stirrup over the saddle horn and reached for the cinch strap. "Spent most of her time in bed. I took care of her."

"You?" she repeated in disbelief.

He glanced at her, then away again, frowning. "Yeah. Me."

"But why didn't your father care for her?"

He snorted in disgust, his bitterness obvious. "He was gone most of the time, supposedly working. But guilt was what kept him away. He was driving the car." He dropped the stirrup from the horn. "Blamed himself for her disability and couldn't live with the guilt, so he avoided it, and her, every chance he got.''

''Who cares for your mother now?''

His frown deepened and he leaned against the horse, bracing his forearms in the saddle's swell. ''Angels,'' he murmured, squinting one eye up at the sky. He stared a moment, as if looking for them, then shook his head and straightened, reaching for the cinch strap. ''My mother's dead. Died about eight years ago.''

Carol watched him strip the saddle from the horse's back. When he turned toward her, she saw in his eyes the misery of the memories that her questions had drawn.

''I better see to my own chores,'' he muttered as he brushed past her.

Carol watched him walk away, wanting to go after him, knowing she shouldn't, and wondering what kind of childhood he could possibly have had, a little boy solely responsible for his invalid mother's care.

Carol finished feeding her horses and stepped from the barn. She paused, catching her lower lip between her teeth, and stole a glance toward the house, wondering if Pete was inside. She hadn't seen him all afternoon, not since he'd helped her unsaddle the horses.

Her every step throughout the afternoon had been haunted by the look on his face, the tightness in his voice when he'd talked about his mother and the bitterness when he'd spoken of his father. Though he'd said that his mother was deceased, her memory lingered, and with it, Carol suspected, a little of his own guilt.

Granted, he'd claimed that his father was the one riddled with guilt, a result of the automobile accident that had left his mother an invalid, but Carol suspected that Pete suffered a little guilt of his own. Why, she wasn't sure. But it was there. She heard it in the gruffness in his voice and saw it in the tautness in his facial features when he spoke of her.

She wavered uncertainly, torn by the desire to talk to him, to learn more about his family, and an equally strong need to put as much distance as possible between them.

Giving in to the former need, she turned for the house.

"Pete?" she called as she opened the back door. She waited, listening for his reply, then stepped into the kitchen. "Pete?" she called again, louder.

She jumped, flattening a hand over her heart, when he stepped from the laundry room on her left, startling her. "Heavens!" she cried, sagging weakly. "You scared the life out of me."

"Sorry," he muttered and brushed past her. "The dryer's running. I didn't hear you come in." He dumped an armload of clothing on the kitchen table, then plucked a T-shirt from the pile to fold, keeping his back to her. "What can I do for you?"

Drawing a deep breath, she dropped her hand to her side and crossed to him. "N-nothing," she said, and picked up a pair of jeans. She shook out the wrinkles, then caught them by the hem, carefully aligning the side seams before folding them in two. "I just finished up at the barn and was about to head

home, but thought I'd stop in and tell you thanks
again, for helping me this morning.''

"No thanks needed. I was glad to help out.''

"Just the same, I—'' She stopped, swallowing
hard as she watched him stuff the folded T-shirt into
the duffel bag propped open on the kitchen chair
beside him. Slowly she lifted her gaze to stare at his
profile. "You're leaving?'' she whispered weakly.

His jaw tightened as he swept another T-shirt
from the pile. "Sooner or later.''

"Did you talk to Clayton?''

"Not yet.'' He folded the shirt quickly, then
stuffed it into the bag. "But I left a message for him
to call me.''

"Then you *are* leaving.''

"I didn't come to stay, Carol,'' he reminded her
dryly. "I only came to help Clayton out for a
while.''

She swept a hand over her hair, holding it back
from her face. "I know that,'' she said, feeling the
panic rising. "It's just that…well, I just didn't expect you to leave so soon.''

"Soon?'' He snorted a laugh as he held two socks
up, checking for a match. "I thought you'd be glad
that I'm leaving.''

"No!'' When he turned to look at her in surprise,
she dropped her hand to her side in frustration, letting her hair fall again to tumble over her shoulders.
"I'm not glad, Pete. But it's for the best.''

"Really?'' he asked, arching a brow. "For who?''

She spun away, lacing her fingers at her waist.
"For both of us.''

"Speak for yourself. I happen to disagree.''

She closed her eyes, digging deep for the strength to keep from turning and throwing herself into his arms. "For me, then," she murmured sadly. She pressed her thumbs together and stared down at them, afraid to look anywhere else. "Pete?"

"What?"

"Did you have a happy childhood?"

"It was okay."

She heard the gruffness in his voice, the hesitancy, the lie, and turned to him. "Caring for an invalid must have been difficult for you."

He scooped the remaining clothes from the table and stuffed them angrily into the bag, unfolded. "I did what I had to do," he muttered, and stalked to the refrigerator.

"What your father should have been doing."

"He couldn't, okay?" he snapped, jerking open the door. "He was the reason she was there and he couldn't stand to face that fact."

"Was he the reason? Or did he simply accept the blame?"

He yanked out a bottle of water and slammed the refrigerator door, turning on her. "How the hell would I know?" he yelled furiously. He twisted off the cap and tipped up the bottle, taking a long drink. He lowered it and dragged the back of his hand across his mouth. "Whatever his reasons, he was never home.

"And I can't say that I blame him," he added, narrowing an eye at her. "Have you ever listened to a woman scream in pain? Listened to her beg for drugs when you knew damn good and well you couldn't give her another one for four more hours?"

He snorted and lifted the bottle again, chugging a drink, then lowered it to point it at her. "It's no wonder the old man never came home. There were times I wished I didn't have to stay there, either." Realizing what he'd admitted, he scowled, then spun and headed for the hallway.

"My father was an alcoholic."

Already through the doorway, Pete stopped. He stood with his back to her a full thirty seconds before he turned to look at her, his eyes narrowed dangerously. "So you had a lousy childhood, too. So what?"

"That's why having roots is so important to me. Why I left you before." She felt the tears rising and gulped them back. "I never lived in the same house for more than six months, or even the same town. Constantly moving, starting over, time after time after time. Watching my father stumble home drunk after drinking up his paycheck. Feeling the sting of his hand when what I wanted, needed, was a hug."

She lifted her hands helplessly as the tears rose and spilled over her lashes. "All I ever dreamed of was escaping. Of having a home. Stability. Roots. A place to call my own. But you didn't want those same things, Pete. That's why I had to end it."

He took a step toward her, then stopped, thinning his lips. "Do you want me to tell you that I've changed?" he growled. "That I feel different now? That I want a wife and a family? Well, I haven't changed. I'm still Pete Dugan," he said, and thumped an angry fist against his chest. "The good-time man, chasing from one rodeo to the next, whooping it up and turning every day into a cowboy

Saturday night.'' Scowling, he flung an impatient hand at her and turned away. ''Go home, Carol,'' he muttered. ''Go back to your house and the roots you want so badly. I'm not the man for you. I never was.''

Seven

Carol closed the truck door behind her and started up the hill behind her house, tears streaming down her face.

Had she set herself up for that last disappointment, she asked herself honestly, or had she been an innocent victim, caught in the crossfire while Pete warred with a past he'd never successfully dealt with?

And she'd thought her own childhood had been rough, she thought, dragging a hand beneath her eyes. Hers had been a walk in the park compared to Pete's. Surrounded by suffering, bearing the responsibility of an invalid's care on child-size shoulders.

Was that what had drawn them to each other in the beginning? The unvoiced miseries of pasts they'd never completely escaped or successfully dealt with? She hiccuped a sob, knowing that even as she asked herself the questions it made no difference now.

Pete was leaving.

Beneath the shade and comfort of the old oak's limbs, she sank to her knees. Dipping her chin to her chest, she pressed a hand to her forehead and gave in to the tears, letting them fall to moisten the dry ground beneath her knees.

Pete stormed around Clayton's bedroom, muttering curses under his breath.

She'd asked for it, he told himself. She'd all but told him to kick her out the door. And it was *she* who had approached him, not the other way around. For his part he hadn't planned on getting anywhere near her. Hadn't he promised himself that very morning that he was getting out of her life and staying out this time? Hadn't he intended to do that very thing up until the very moment he'd seen her unloading those handicapped kids at the arena?

Swearing, he whirled, and paced in the opposite direction, rubbing a hand across the back of his neck.

It wasn't too late, he told himself. He could still make good his promise. He could still leave. He could get out of her life and stay out for good.

But first, he told himself as he headed for the door, he was going to apologize to her one last time for hurting her.

Pete drew in a deep breath, then lifted his fist to rap on the door. He waited, glancing up at the sky where the sun was already making its slow descent. When his knock drew no response, he lowered his gaze to frown at the closed door.

She was home. He knew she was. He'd parked his truck on the drive right behind hers.

He opened the screen and tried the knob. Discovering it was unlocked, he twisted it and pushed open the door, taking a hesitant step inside. "Carol?"

When she didn't answer, he took another step into the room and glanced around. "Carol?"

He waited, listening, but still didn't hear a sound. Feeling like a burglar or, at the very least, a snoop, he turned back for the door, intending to leave, but stopped when his gaze struck a picture placed on top of the console television. Crossing the room, he picked up the framed picture to look at it, his heart tightening as he confirmed his suspicion. It was a picture of him, riding Honey—or rather Twister—at the Finals. The picture was one of thousands he'd seen in print, distributed by the company whose products he endorsed.

But why did Carol have one? he wondered in confusion. And why did she have it out on display? Especially considering she'd ended their relationship more than two years ago? Didn't women burn all reminders of past relationships? Or at least hide them?

Setting the picture down, he turned and crossed to the kitchen, unable to stem his curiosity. He stopped just inside the doorway and simply stared. Yellow-and-white gingham curtains hung at the high window above the sink, framing pots of herbs that lined the sill. A solitary bowl and spoon set in the drainboard, washed and placed there to dry, he was sure, after a breakfast she'd eaten alone that morning.

Home, he remembered her saying. That's what she'd always wanted, and it seemed that's what she'd created for herself, he thought as he glanced slowly around the room, noting the framed floral prints hanging on the wall, the three-tiered shelf lined with a collection of old pottery, and the drop-leaf table covered with an embroidered cloth.

It felt like home, he realized. Even to him, a man who had never had a desire for one.

He froze when his gaze settled on a vase of wild-flowers, placed on the table's center, their stems drooping over the twisted strip of rawhide that held them together, their once-colorful blooms faded, fallen ones scattered like confetti around the vase's base.

She'd kept his miserable little peace offering for two days, long past the flowers' glory, he thought, touched by the sentimentality in that gesture. He should have bought her roses, dozens of them, he told himself, and had them delivered to her front door. He could well afford the extravagance. And Carol deserved more than a bouquet of wildflowers plucked from a field.

His mouth suddenly dry, he moved to the sink and pulled a glass from the cupboard. Holding it beneath the tap, he turned on the water and lifted his face to peer through the window as the glass filled.

And saw her.

Kneeling beneath the old oak tree, her shoulders

stooped, her head bowed. He watched, swallowing hard, his Adam's apple bobbing as her shoulders heaved convulsively.

She was crying.

And he was the one who'd caused the tears.

Turning for the door, he jerked it open and leaped over the porch steps, clearing them in one jump, then ran up the small hill, ignoring the pain in his knee. He slowed as he neared her, his approach unnoticed, concealed by the sound of her gentle weeping.

His breath burning in his lungs, he dropped to a knee behind her and placed a hand on her shoulder. "Carol?"

She tensed at his touch, then whirled to face him, her eyes wide with fear. When she turned, Pete saw the granite marker that her body had concealed from him before that moment.

A tombstone? He didn't remember a tombstone being beneath the tree before. He frowned, staring at it as the words chiseled on the gray granite slowly came into focus.

Infant son of Carol Benson
Born July 16, 1998
Loved, but never forgotten.

The fingers he'd rested on her shoulder curled, digging into her skin as he did the math. A son. Carol had given birth to a son. *His* son, he thought, feeling the shock, the anger, the grief swell inside him, fighting for dominance. He'd never known. Never known.

Slowly he turned to look at her, needing her confirmation, and saw the guilt in her tear-filled eyes, the fear. "We had a son?" he whispered, his voice raw. "A son?"

"Y-yes," she cried brokenly.

"You never told me."

"I wanted to," she said miserably, then dipped her chin, pressing trembling fingers against her lips. "I wanted to, Pete," she said desperately, lifting her face to his. "I swear I wanted to."

He rose slowly, his gaze riveted on hers, his facial muscles growing hard, his eyes turning dark and unforgiving. Then he spun and stalked away.

She hadn't thought he'd make a suitable father.

That thought ate on Pete during the drive back to Clayton's ranch until fury paced like a wild animal inside him. Hell, he thought as he braked to a dust-churning stop in front of Clayton's house and shot the gearshift into Park. He knew as well as she did that he wouldn't have made a suitable father. But he'd had a son, dammit! A son! Didn't he have a right to know about that? Shouldn't she at least have informed him of the fact?

Angry, he climbed down from the truck and slammed the door behind him. Bracing his hands low on his hips, he drew in a deep breath and let his head fall back, the grief swelling from deep inside him, a pain so ripe and debilitating that it finally dragged him to his knees.

A son. He'd had a son.

Tears burned behind his eyes, and he didn't even

try to stop them. Bowing his head, he dropped his face into his hands and wept.

"Is Pete going to watch me ride today?"

Hoping to hide the emotions that hearing Pete's name drew, Carol turned her face away. "No, not today, Adam."

"Is he still here?"

She straightened and saw that Adam was standing up in the stirrups, straining to look toward the house. "I guess so," she said vaguely, then ducked her head to check the cinch. "His truck's still here."

"How do you know he's not? Did he tell you so?"

"No, but I'm sure he's got things to do."

"Like what?"

She huffed a breath. "I don't know," she said, her frustration, as well as her impatience, growing. "But I'm sure he has chores."

"Can I go and ask him?"

She snapped up her head. "Ask him?" she repeated dully.

"Yeah," he said, glancing down at her, then back toward the house. "I bet he'd even ride with me again. He likes riding Honey."

"I don't know, Adam. He's probably busy—"

"There he is!" he squealed. "Pete!" he yelled, waving an arm excitedly over his head. "Over here! It's me, Adam!"

Though she had to force herself to do so, Carol turned in time to see Pete stop at the sound of Adam's voice and glance over in their direction. He lifted a hand and waved, returning Adam's smile.

But his smile slipped into a frown when he shifted his gaze to Carol's.

"Wanna ride with me again?" Adam called out to him.

Carol could see Pete's hesitation, even understand it, then nearly choked when she saw him head their way.

"I might," Pete said, resting a hand on Adam's knee as he grinned up at the boy. "In fact, I was just heading out to the far pasture to check on a cow who's close to calving. How about you and me making that ride together?"

Adam whipped his head around to look at Carol, his eyes full of excitement and hope. "Could I, Miss Carol? Please?"

"I don't know, Adam," she began hesitantly, then had to leap back out of the way when Pete swung up behind Adam, nearly striking her on the nose with his boot as he dropped his leg over the opposite side. She glared up at him angrily.

"You don't have to worry," he said tersely. "I can be trusted to take care of the kid."

She clamped her lips together, swallowing back the arguments, the warnings she'd been ready to voice. "Fine," she snapped. She spun and headed for the barn. "Pete's the boss, Adam," she called over her shoulder. "Mind what he says."

"Yes, ma'am," she heard the boy reply, then his squeal of delight when Pete goosed Honey into a lope and the two raced away.

Pete wasn't sure what had possessed him to take Adam up on his offer, though he had a number of reasons to choose from. First, he knew his agreement to ride with the boy was sure to make Carol mad, an opportunity he found hard to resist. Second, the chance to be around the boy again was tempting. He was a cute kid, a little green around horses yet, but he had the desire, the determination…and maybe a little wild streak that Pete remembered from his own childhood. And third, if he was honest, Pete had to admit that he'd wanted the chance to test his fathering skills, just to see if they were as bad as Carol must have thought when she'd elected not to tell him about her pregnancy.

He leaned his ear close to the boy's to be heard over the wind rushing by their heads. "Slow her down a little," he instructed, then closed his hands over Adam's on the reins to make sure the boy did so gently and without jerking on the horse's mouth. When Honey had settled into a brisk trot, he lifted an arm and pointed. "See that herd of cattle over there?"

Adam followed the direction of Pete's finger. "Yeah. I see 'em."

"Head that way. The cow we need to check is in that herd."

Adam reined the horse in the direction of the cattle. "How do you know which one is about to calve?" he asked curiously. "There's so many."

"Oh," Pete said expansively, and wondered how far he should go with an explanation. He wasn't sure he wanted to turn this ride into a sex education class. "It's not so hard, really," he said, deciding to take the safe route. "Just look for a fat one."

Adam frowned, studying the cattle intently, then

cocked his head over his shoulder to look at Pete.
"But they're all fat."

Pete tossed back his head and laughed at the se-
riousness of the expression on the boy's tipped up
face. "Gotcha," he said, grinning, and poked Adam
playfully in the ribs. He lifted his head, still grinning, and looked toward the cattle again. "There're
ways, though. A mama cow who is close to her time
has a bigger belly. Low and full, hanging closer to
the ground. And her teats are full, too," he added.
He leaned around Adam to peer at the boy. "You
ever blown up a rubber glove like you would a bal-
loon?"

At Adam's nod he said, "Well, that's what the
mama cow's bag looks like." He held out his hand,
stretching his fingers as wide apart as he could.
"Kinda like this," he said, demonstrating. Dropping
his hand to his thigh again, he nodded his head toward the cattle. "Now work your way real slow
through the herd and see if you can pick out the
mama cow."

Adam looked left and right as he guided Honey
through the herd, his forehead wrinkled in concen-
tration. "That one?" he asked uncertainly, pointing
as he reined Honey to a stop.

"Nope. Her bag's not full enough. See?" Pete
said, pointing beneath the cow. "It's limp, the teats
almost hanging straight down. No milk there."

Pursing his lips in determination, Adam urged
Honey on. He studied the cattle as if his very life
depended on finding that mama cow, a fact that
drew a smile from Pete.

"That one," Adam announced firmly, stopping

Honey again. The cow he pointed to stopped grazing and swung her head around to peer at them as she slowly chewed.

Pete smiled proudly. "That's the one, all right." He dropped a hand on Adam's shoulder and squeezed. "You're going to make a fine rancher someday."

Adam beamed at the praise. "Now what?"

"Well, it looks to me like the mama cow is doing okay, and she's not ready to drop that calf, yet, so I guess we get to goof off for a while. How long does your riding lesson usually last, anyway?"

"Two hours. My mom will be back to pick me up at eleven."

Pete glanced at his wristwatch. "I'd say we've got time, then."

"For what?" Adam asked curiously.

"Ever been to Clayton's private hole?"

Adam wrinkled his nose. "What hole?"

"His swimming hole." He waved a hand. "Head Honey on up to that stand of oaks just ahead and I'll show you."

"Are we going swimming?" Adam asked, his eyes going round.

"Well, heck, yeah!" Pete said in surprise. "You don't think I'd show you Clayton's private hole only to let you look at it, do you?"

"Hot dog!" Adam cried, and squeezed his legs against Honey's side, urging her into a fast trot.

"Pete?"

Drugged by the warmth of the sun that dried his damp skin, Pete kept his eyes closed beneath his cowboy hat and hummed a lazy response. "Hmmm?"

"Do you have any kids?"

Pete tensed, then forced his shoulders to relax. "Nope. Do you?"

Adam giggled. "No, silly. I'm not old enough."

"Last I heard, there weren't any age requirements."

"There's not?"

"Nope." He uncrossed his legs, then recrossed them, switching his right leg to cross over his left. "You have to pass a test, though," he added.

"What kind of test?"

"A daddy test."

"What's a daddy test?"

"Oh, it's a tough one. You gotta be able to climb tall buildings, jump through fire without getting burned, and you gotta be able to hold your breath for at least eight minutes."

"Hold your breath? Why?"

Pete tipped up his hat to look at the boy. "How else is a man supposed to survive changing a dirty diaper?"

Adam stared at him, his forehead puckered in doubt, then laughed and poked at Pete's bare chest. "You're pulling my leg."

Pete swiped a finger over his heart, making an X. "Serious as a heart attack. That's why I don't have any kids. I fail that breath-holding test every time." He dropped his hat back over his eyes and shifted his shoulders on the grass, trying to find a more comfortable position. "Came close that last time, though," he added. "Made it seven minutes and thirty seconds before I passed out cold."

Adam laughed, and the sound drew a smile to Pete's lips, then the boy sighed and drew up his knees, wrapping his skinny arms around his legs. "I wish you were my daddy," the boy muttered wistfully.

The smile that had curved Pete's lips quickly melted. "Don't you have a daddy?" he asked quietly.

"No—well, sorta."

Pete lifted his hat again to peer at the boy. "How do you 'sorta' have a daddy?"

Adam dropped his gaze, frowning, and dug a finger in the dirt. "My mama and daddy are divorced. They're supposed to share custody of me, but my daddy moved to Indiana, so I never hardly see him anymore."

"That's tough, kid," he offered quietly. "You must miss him a lot."

Adam lifted a shoulder. "Not really. He was hardly ever around before, anyways."

Slowly Pete sat up, hooking his hat over a propped knee. "My daddy wasn't around much, either," he admitted quietly.

Adam cocked his head to look over at him. "He wasn't?"

"Nope," Pete said, and frowned at the brim of his hat. "Worked all the time. But I made out all right without him," he added, shooting Adam an encouraging wink.

"Yeah. Me, too. Though sometimes I wish he was around so I could talk to him. Man stuff," he explained when Pete looked at him quizzically. "There's just some stuff my mom doesn't understand."

"Like what?" Pete asked curiously.

"Like sports. I want to play baseball, but my mom won't let me." He pushed his lips into a pout. "She's afraid I'll get hurt," he said wryly. He poked a finger at the bridge of his glasses. "Because of these," he muttered. "She says I could get hit in the face, or something, and they'd break, scarring me for life, and maybe making me blind."

Pete stared at Adam a moment, unable to believe anyone lived with those kinds of fears, or would force them onto a little boy. Then he tossed back his head and laughed and leaned to ruffle the boy's hair. "Your mom worries because she loves you."

"Loves me?" Adam snorted a disbelieving breath. "Yeah, right."

"No, she really does," Pete insisted. "If she didn't, she wouldn't care if you got hurt."

"Maybe," Adam replied doubtfully.

Pete frowned as he stared at the boy, a thought occurring to him. "If she won't let you play baseball, how in the world did you ever talk her into letting you take horseback riding lessons?"

Adam lifted his shoulder again. "I wouldn't have, if it weren't for Miss Carol. Mama cuts her hair. Miss Carol talked Mama into trading her haircuts for private lessons. Mama finally agreed, 'cause she likes Miss Carol and trusts her to keep me safe."

Which explained Carol's panic when Honey ran away with Adam, Pete thought, and why she'd been hesitant in allowing Adam to go with him today. But haircuts in exchange for private horseback riding lessons? He frowned, knowing damn good and well there was no way Carol could get enough haircuts in five years or more to balance out the cost of the private horseback riding lessons she was giving Adam.

Shaking his head, he pushed himself to his feet and settled his hat over his head. "We better be heading back," he said, glancing at his wristwatch. "It's getting close to eleven."

Reluctantly Adam dragged himself to his feet. "Do we have to?" he complained.

Pete chuckled and scooped Adam's cap from the ground and jammed it down over the boy's ears. "Now, what would your mom do if she showed up at the ranch and you weren't there?"

Scowling, Adam bumped the brim of the cap, shoving it back on his head. "Worry."

"Right," Pete agreed, and unwound Honey's reins from the limb he'd tied them to earlier. "And if she starts worrying about you riding horses, then she's liable to put an end to the lessons, right?"

"Right," Adam agreed grudgingly.

Pete cupped his hands, offering Adam a boost up into the saddle. After the boy had settled, Pete plucked his shirt from the saddle horn and tied the sleeves around his waist. "I have an idea," he said on sudden inspiration as he swung up behind Adam.

Adam turned the reins against Honey's neck, heading the horse for home. "What?"

"Well, your mother won't let you play baseball,

but do you think she'd allow you to throw the ball around some at home?''

Adam snorted. ''With who? Her? My mom's a girl. She doesn't know how to throw a ball.''

''Well, I wouldn't be so sure about that,'' Pete was quick to correct. ''There's a lot of women around who can throw a ball better than most men. But what I was thinking,'' he went on, ''is that maybe you and me could throw the ball around some.''

Adam whipped his head around to look at Pete, the eyes behind the thick glasses wide. ''You'd do that?''

''Well, sure,'' Pete said. ''But you'll have to understand that I'm not around a lot. I'm on the road a good bit of the time, rodeoing. But when I'm in the area, I could drop by and we could hit some balls. Maybe even take some more horseback rides together. Clayton's a friend of mine, and I know he'd let me borrow a horse.''

''I bet Carol'd let you borrow Honey,'' Adam offered helpfully.

At the mention of Carol, Pete frowned, realizing he'd just committed himself into the probability of seeing her again in the future. ''We'll see,'' he murmured vaguely.

Carol paced in the barn doorway, casting an occasional glance toward the pasture and the gate Pete and Adam had passed through earlier when they'd left to check on the cow. She glanced at her watch and groaned, realizing that Adam's mother would be arriving at any minute and knowing the woman would have a conniption fit when she discovered that Carol had allowed Adam to leave with Pete.

Wringing her hands, she paced away, then back again, lifting her gaze to the gate. She sagged with relief when she saw Honey approaching, looking small in the distance, but definitely carrying two people on her back.

She walked out into the barnyard to wait for them and bit back a moan when she heard the sound of a car engine. Casting a quick glance to her left, she saw Amanda's car approaching. She forced a smile and lifted a hand in greeting as Amanda pulled to a stop a short distance away.

Amanda shot from the car, her eyes wide with panic. "Where's Adam? Is he all right? Has there been an accident?"

Carol placed a calming hand on the woman's arm. "He's fine. He's just out on a ride." She lifted her hand to point toward the gate. "See? There he is now."

Amanda whirled, her eyes going wider. "Alone? You allowed him to ride alone?"

"No," Carol replied, struggling for patience. "Pete's with him."

"Pete?" she cried, turning back to stare at Carol, her worries in no way absolved. "Who is Pete?"

"Pete Dugan. A friend of Clayton's. He's here looking after things while Clayton and Rena are gone."

Amanda laced her fingers together and twisted them in a knot as she turned back to watch the horse's slow approach. "This Pete person, he is a skilled rider, isn't he?" she asked uneasily.

Carol rolled her eyes as she moved to stand beside her. "Yes, he's a skilled rider," she assured the woman. "I wouldn't have allowed Adam to go with him if he wasn't."

Amanda placed a hand over her brow, shading her eyes, and her mouth dropped open. "Why, he doesn't have on a shirt!" she cried in dismay.

Carol strained to see. "Who? Adam?"

"No! The man riding behind him."

At that moment Pete swung down from the saddle and landed nimbly on the ground, then headed for the gate to open it, giving Carol—and Adam's mother—a clearer view of his bare chest.

"He probably just got hot," Carol said, hoping to soothe the woman's offended sensibilities.

At that moment Adam caught sight of his mother and shouted a greeting, waving a hand over his head. Pete glanced up, then away and swung back up behind Adam. He leaned to whisper something in the boy's ear. The breeze carried Adam's delighted laughter to the two women who waited impatiently for the boy's return.

"Well, Adam certainly seems to be enjoying the man's company," Amanda commented in surprise.

Carol lifted a shoulder. "Pete's a fun guy." She forced a smile as the riders drew near. "Did you have a good time, Adam?" she called out to him.

"I had a blast!" Adam cried, though the broad smile he wore was answer enough. He reined Honey to a stop and Pete slid down from the horse's back, then held up his arms to help Adam down.

Pete turned then, and avoided looking at Carol by offering Amanda a smile and a hand in greeting.

"How do, ma'am," he said politely. "I'm Pete Dugan."

Amanda took the offered hand, her cheeks going pink as she forced her gaze from his bare chest and to his face. "P-pleased to meet you, Pete," she stammered. "I'm Amanda, Adam's mother."

Pete shot her a wink and grinned as he untied his shirt from around his waist. "Figured you were. Adam talked quite a bit about you."

Amanda arched a brow and looked down at her son. "He did?" she asked in surprise.

"Yep," Pete said. "The boy's a regular chatterbox." He shrugged the shirt on, then draped an arm around Adam's shoulders without bothering to button it. "While we were out riding, we discovered that we have a lot of interests in common. Isn't that right, Adam?" he asked, glancing down at the boy.

Adam grinned up at him. "Sure do."

"Like what?" Amanda asked in astonishment.

"Horses, for one," Pete replied, and graced her with one of his most winning smiles. "And baseball, too." When he saw her mouth drop open and was sure that she was going to start sputtering denials about Adam's interest in the sport, he interjected quickly, "In fact," he said, growing serious, "I was wanting to ask your permission to drop by your house sometime, so that Adam and I could throw a ball around." He tightened his arm around Adam's shoulders and drew the boy against his side. "Being on the road so much, I don't have the opportunity to play much ball, but I sure love the game. I'd consider it a personal favor if you'd allow me the pleasure of playing some with Adam when I'm in town.''

Carol stood frozen, unable to believe she was hearing this conversation. Pete play baseball? She wasn't even aware that he knew home plate from left field.

Certain that Amanda—considering how overprotective the single mother was—would never agree to such an offer, especially from a stranger, a man she'd only just met, Carol glanced in the woman's direction and was stunned to hear her reply, ''Well, yes, I guess that'd be all right.''

Pete opened up the Yellow Pages across his spread knees and flipped through the pages. Finding the section he wanted, he ran a finger down the list of businesses listed there.

''Ornamental Stone and Monuments,'' he muttered. Picking up the phone, he checked the number again, then quickly punched it in.

Inhaling deeply, he placed the phone to his ear and listened to it ring. ''Yes, sir,'' he replied to the man who answered his call. ''I wonder if I might ask you a few questions.''

Eight

"No, I haven't been able to get ahold of Clayton, and his hired hand's laid up in the hospital. His chicken pox took a turn for the worse." Pete tipped the phone away from his mouth to take a sip from a bottle of chilled water as he waited for Troy's reply.

"I can come and relieve you," Troy said after a moment. "But I can't get there for four or five days. Yuma and me are headed for Wyoming, then winding our way back down south, planning to hit a couple of rodeos on the return trip to Texas."

Pete rubbed the bottle against his bare chest, letting the condensation cool his skin, hot after the shower he'd just taken. He bit back a sigh, trying to hide his frustration from Troy, as well as his desperation to get the hell off Clayton's ranch. "That's good enough," he said, and moved to stand in front of the bedroom window. "Just don't dally too long."

"Is something wrong?" Troy asked, his voice holding a note of suspicion.

Pete watched Carol step from the barn, one shoulder stooped beneath the weight of the feed bucket she carried. "No," he lied, and dragged the bottle across his forehead, hoping to ease the ache there. "I'm just anxious to get back on the road. I've already missed too many rodeos."

"You're still in the top ten, though," Troy assured him. "I checked the rankings myself less than an hour ago."

"What about you?" Pete asked, hoping to switch the conversation before it slipped into an area he didn't want to discuss. "How've you been doing?"

He heard the defeat in the sigh that crossed through the airwaves. "Not so good," Troy admitted reluctantly. "Still haven't managed to pick up any prize money."

"Are you throwing any?" Pete asked in concern, knowing how a long, dry spell could affect a cowboy's confidence.

"Yeah, I've thrown a few, but not fast enough to place. Yuma's doing good, though," he added quickly, and Pete could well imagine the proud smile spreading across his friend's face. Troy was a good sport, never resenting a competitor's better time or holding it against the other man. And the congratulations he offered to those who beat him out of a chance at any prize money was always sincere and delivered straight from the heart. Troy was just that kind of guy. He lived by the Cowboy Code, and served as a good example to the younger steer wrestlers stepping into the professional ranks for the first time.

"Your luck's bound to change soon," Pete assured him. "You're due a win."

"Yeah," Troy said, chuckling ruefully. "That's what you said the last time we talked."

"Well, it's true," Pete insisted. "You just keep your focus. You'll do all right."

"What about you?" Troy asked. "How are you and Carol getting along?"

Pete frowned as he stared at the woman in question through the bedroom window as she went about her chores at the barn. "We're staying out of each other's way," he replied noncommittally.

"But last time we talked, I thought you said that things were—"

"Listen, Troy," Pete said, interrupting him before he was forced to respond to any questions he didn't have the answers to. "I'm going to have to run. I've got to drive into town and pick up some oats for Clayton before the feed store closes. You take care, hear?"

"Yeah, and you do the same," Troy said, then broke the connection.

Blowing out a long breath of relief, Pete punched the disconnect button on his cell phone and tossed it to the bed. Turning back to the window, he folded his arms across his chest and watched Carol step inside the barn. A sense of loss filled him as he watched her disappear inside the barn's shadowed interior. Slowly he rubbed the bottle across his chest and over his heart.

"Yeah, I'll take care," he murmured under his breath. "But the only way I'm going to be able to do that is to get the hell out of here."

The errand to the feed store hadn't been a total lie. Pete really did need to pick up a load of oats for Clayton. But the sense of urgency he'd implied to Troy wasn't just a stretch of the truth. It was a bald-faced lie. The supply of oats in the barn would last another couple of days, maybe even a week, if Pete stretched it a bit.

Just the same, he climbed into his truck and headed for the highway, needing to put some distance between Carol and himself, if only for the hour or so it took to make the drive to town and back.

Reaching for the buttons that lined the dash, he punched one, and country music filled the cab of his truck. The song playing was an old one of George Strait's and one that never failed to draw a smile from Pete. "All My Exes Live in Texas." He chuckled, then puckered his lips and began to whistle an accompaniment to the singing.

He saw a truck parked on the highway's shoulder ahead, caution lights flashing, the hood propped up. The cheerful tune died on his lips as he recognized the truck as Carol's. "Oh, no," he muttered as he eased his boot off the accelerator. Tempted to drive right on past, he frowned and whipped the wheel to the right, pulled up behind her and turned off his engine.

Leaning a shoulder against the door, he opened it

and dropped to the ground. At the sound of the door closing, Carol's face appeared around the front end of her truck, then quickly disappeared again.

His frown deepened. Obviously, she wasn't any more anxious than he was for another confrontation. Knowing he couldn't leave her stranded, though, he strode for the front of her truck. "What's the problem?" he asked, stopping beside her.

Her head was buried beneath the hood and muffled her mumbled reply even more. "Fuel line's clogged, I think."

He gave her hip a nudge with his, shoving her out of the way, and dipped his head over the engine, poking a finger at the tangle of wires. "What's it doing?"

Carol folded her arms across her chest, angry that she needed his help and resenting his take-charge attitude. "Sputtering. Hits about fifty, then starts losing speed. If I take my foot off the gas, the engine dies."

"Sounds like the fuel line to me," he agreed as he pulled his head from beneath the raised hood. He braced his hands along the edge of the engine and leaned forward, pondering the problem, then cocked his head over his shoulder to look back at her. "Nothing we can do to repair it here. I'm headed for town. Do you want a tow?"

"I've got my cell phone. I can call a wrecker."

"Yeah, you could, and fork over some hard-earned cash. *Or*," he added pointedly, "you could let me give you a free tow."

He watched her waver, shifting her weight from

one foot to the other, and knew she didn't want to accept his offer of help.

After a moment she heaved a breath. "All right," she said grudgingly. "I've got a tow chain in the back of the truck."

She spun to retrieve it, and Pete pulled down the hood, pressing his palms against it to lock it into place. Sighing, he turned to follow her. "Here," he said, taking the chain from her. "I'll hook it up. You'll just get dirty."

"And you won't?" she argued stubbornly, maintaining a firm grip on one end of the chain.

"No," he said, struggling for patience. "I'll probably get just as dirty as you, but I can't stand by and watch a woman do a job better suited to a man." Giving the chain a yank, he ripped it from her grasp and strode angrily for the front of her truck again, cursing her under his breath with every step. Dropping down to the ground, he rolled to his back and scooted beneath the truck to hook the chain to the front axle. Checking the connection and ensuring it would hold, he shimmied his way from beneath the truck, rolled to his feet and stood, dusting off his hands.

Glancing up, he saw her standing where he'd left her, her mouth pursed, her back stiff, her arms folded stubbornly across her breasts. Biting back a sigh, he walked toward her. "I'll pull my truck around in front of yours. If it'll make you feel any better, you can crawl underneath this time and hook up the chain to my truck."

"Why, thank you," she replied sarcastically, then

huffed a fuming breath and marched to the front of her truck, pumping her arms angrily at her sides.

In spite of his frustration with her, Pete found himself chuckling as he climbed back into his truck. Carol Benson was one stubborn lady. And when she had a bee in her bonnet... He shook his head and laughed as he started the engine. Well, it was better to just steer clear.

He pulled around in front of her truck, then reversed, watching in the rearview mirror for her to signal for him to stop. When she did, he threw the gearshift into Park, and slumped down in the seat, waiting. Moments later she appeared on the passenger side, her face red, her hair wild. She yanked open the door and climbed inside, flopping down on the seat. She jerked the seat belt across her and clicked it into position, then fell back against the seat and folded her arms across her chest as she turned her face to glare at the windshield.

"You've got grease on your cheek."

Scowling, she slapped a hand against the sun visor, folding it down, then sat up to peer at her reflection in the vanity mirror attached to the visor's underside. Seeing the grease, she glanced about, looking for something to wipe it away with.

Noting her problem, Pete lifted a hip and pulled a handkerchief from his rear pocket. "Here," he said, handing it to her. "Use this."

She looked at the scrap of white he offered, her reluctance to accept anything from him obvious, then snatched it from his hand. "Thanks," she muttered ungraciously as she scrubbed furiously at her cheek.

Grinning, Pete sank back against his seat and just watched. "You're welcome."

She snapped her head around to frown at him. "Well?" she asked expectantly. "Are we leaving or not?"

Pete's grin widened. "I suppose we could," he said slowly and cast a glance in his rearview mirror, then at her again. "But who's gonna steer your truck and work the brakes while I tow it?"

Groaning, her cheeks flaming in embarrassment, Carol grabbed for the door handle and shoved open the door. "Me," she muttered, and slammed the door behind her.

"How long?" Pete asked as Carol climbed into his truck.

"They're going to call me later, after they have a chance to look at it more closely. Might be a couple of days, though," she said, trying to avoid his gaze. "They have to order a part."

She clipped on her seat belt, then turned her face to the passenger window.

On the glass Pete had a perfect reflection of her face and the tears that gleamed in her eyes. "Bad news?" he asked softly.

"It could be worse," she replied, then dashed a finger beneath her nose.

"How much?" Pete asked, suspecting it was the cost of the repair that was causing her current state of distress.

"Enough."

"Five hundred?"

"No."

"High or low?"

She huffed a breath and picked up his handkerchief from the seat to blow her nose. "Low," she murmured miserably, pressing the cloth beneath her nose. "More like a thousand."

"Can you cover it?"

She nodded tearfully, unable to voice a reply, then drew in a deep breath and lifted her chin, wadding the handkerchief into a ball against her thigh. "It'll take a chunk out of my savings, but I'll manage."

Pete shook his head. "You could probably manage better if you'd charge a fair price for all those horseback riding lessons you give."

"How I run my business is *no* business of yours," she replied resentfully.

Something inside Pete snapped at her continued stubbornness and brought back his own resentment toward her. "No, but having a son sure as hell was," he said furiously, and ripped down the gearshift. He whipped the truck back out onto the street and took the corner too fast, rocking the truck to two wheels.

Carol braced a hand against the dash and snapped her head around to glare at him. "Stop this truck right this instant."

"Why?" he goaded and increased the speed. "Are you planning on getting out and walking home?"

"No, but I certainly intend to arrive in one piece. Now stop!"

Setting his jaw, Pete whipped the truck into the parking lot of a vacant building and stomped on the brake, throwing Carol hard against her seat belt. He shoved up the gearshift and switched off the ignition, then whirled in his seat to face her. "Okay," he growled. "I stopped. Now what?"

"I'll tell you what!" she replied, seething. "We are going to have this out once and for all. Right here. Right now," she said, stabbing a finger against the seat. Her eyes flashing angrily, she unfastened her seat belt and flung it back, spinning around in her seat to face him. "No, I didn't tell you about the baby," she said, each word a serrated knife against her throat as she pushed them past the tears that clogged it. "That was selfish and wrong of me, and I've apologized. More than once.

"But what if I *had* told you, Pete?" she demanded angrily, neatly turning the tables on him. "What would you have done? Danced some fancy two-step, then run in the opposite direction as fast as you could when I wasn't looking? Or would you have offered to marry me, as Clayton did to Rena, then spent the rest of your life on the road, avoiding me, the way he has his wife?"

She flopped back against the passenger door and folded her arms over her chest, her eyes riveted on his. "Which would it have been, Pete? Huh?" she prodded viciously. "Run or a shotgun marriage? I've often wondered what you'd have done if I had told you about the baby, and I think that right now I'd really like to hear your answer."

Pete stared at her, his eyes narrowed dangerously, the fury that raged through him making his blood burn through his veins. "You don't think very much of me, do you?" he grated out.

She choked on a laugh. "To be honest," she replied haughtily, "I try not to think of you at all."

The hand that streaked across the distance that separated them shot out so fast Carol didn't have time to dodge it. By the time she did become aware of it, it was already fisted in her blouse and she was being hauled across the console until her nose was bare inches from Pete's, his breath like a blowtorch on her face.

"You offered only two choices, Carol," he reminded her, his voice deadly calm. "You never considered for one minute that I might have *wanted* to marry you, that I might have worked *hard* at being a good husband to you and a father to our son."

She gulped, swallowed, trying to still the frantic pounding of her heart, to tamp down the wild hope that surged, pushing tears into her eyes. "You're right, Pete," she said, her voice trembling, "I didn't. So now you have three choices. Which one would you have made?"

Carol lay in her bed, staring at the ceiling, the sheet drawn to her chin. She lifted it to dab at her eyes, then lowered it again, clutching it to her chest.

Three choices. Easy, really, to choose one of the three and offer it up to Carol to finally put her mind at ease.

But had he?

A sob rose in her throat and she choked it back, as she had every other sob that had risen since she'd crawled into her bed.

No. He hadn't made a choice. He'd stared at her, his eyes dark with accusation, his fingers knotted in her blouse, forcing her to remain close to him, to meet his gaze, until she had been sure she would scream from the nerve-wrenching suspense, while she waited for him to give her his answer.

Then he'd shoved her, pushing her back into her seat, and had reached for the key, starting the engine. With her slumped in the seat beside him, staring at him through a flood of tears, he'd driven her home. He had braked to a rough stop in front of her house and sat with his eyes narrowed on the windshield in front of him while he waited for her to get out. Never once during the ride did he look her way. Never once did he speak a word to her.

Never once did he reveal his choice.

The following night Carol was standing at her kitchen window when she saw the twin beams of headlights streaking up the hill behind her house. Knowing the lights meant someone was coming up her drive from the opposite direction, she dropped the dish cloth and headed for the back door. She stepped out onto the porch and waited, squinting against the glare of bright headlights headed toward her, and recognized the truck as Pete's.

Wondering what would bring him to her house, and especially at this hour of the night, she ran down the steps and hurried to the edge of the yard to meet him. As he pulled the truck up beside her, he leaned across the seat and shoved open the passenger door. Dirt, riding in the back, planted his paws on the side of the truck's bed and barked a greeting.

"Get in," Pete ordered gruffly.

Frowning, she took a step back. "Look, Pete," she said, her temper rising. "You're not giving me any more orders, understand?"

"Get in!" he repeated, yelling the command this time.

Startled by the anger in his voice, the desperation, she stepped to the door, opening it wide as she climbed inside. Before she could even close the door, he was spinning the steering wheel and making a wild U-turn and tearing back out her drive.

"Pete!" she cried, bracing a hand against the dash. "What on earth is wrong with you? You're going to kill us!"

"Cattle are out," he said through tight lips, his gaze focused on the road ahead. "Somebody knocked down a section of fence. They're scattered all up and down the highway. A car's already hit one of 'em. Cops are swarming all over the place, but they don't have a clue how to herd cattle. They've spooked 'em, scattering 'em to hell and back."

Sobering, Carol stared through the windshield, envisioning the mass confusion, the danger involved for motorists on the dark highway and to the cattle who roamed it. "We'll need horses," she murmured, thinking out loud, then glanced behind her at Dirt who had his nose pressed against the rear window. "And Dirt can help."

"That's why I brought him."

A siren's wail split the night, and Carol whipped her head back around, her eyes wide. They topped the hill, and she clapped a hand over her mouth, smothering the moan that rose. "Oh, my God!" she cried, shocked by the scene that came into view. The flashing red lights, people milling all over the highway, cattle bawling, darting in and out of the beams of swirling light, their eyes rolling, panicked and not sure which way to run.

Swearing, Pete veered the truck toward the shoulder, slammed on the brakes and hopped out. Carol was right behind him.

"Turn off the damn lights," he yelled, gesturing wildly at the state troopers gathered in the middle of the highway. "You're spooking the cattle."

One of the troopers snorted and turned to grin at one of his partners. "Who the hell does he think he is?" he said with a jerk of his chin toward Pete. "Wyatt Earp?"

Pete strode straight for the man who'd made the wisecrack and stuck his nose in the guy's face. "No, I'm Pete Dugan, and I sure as hell know more about rounding up cattle than you do. Now shut off that damn siren and cut the lights."

Carol cut a nervous glance toward Pete as she untied the two horses Pete had already unloaded from the trailer and tied to its rear gate, sure that at any moment fists would start flying. She recognized the trooper and headed toward him and Pete, tugging the horses behind her.

"Hey, Jim," she said, forcing a smile. "We really appreciate y'all's help, but we can handle it from here."

The man she'd spoken to tore his gaze from Pete's to peer at her. "Carol?"

"Yeah, it's me," she said, and turned up the wattage on her smile. "I know Clayton will want to thank you himself for your help, when he gets back in town. I'll be sure and tell him that you guys responded quickly and efficiently to avoid a sure crisis.''

Jim shifted his gaze to Pete's again and scowled, obviously not wanting to be the first to back down.

To facilitate the end of the face-off, Carol nudged a set of reins into Pete's hand. "Come on, Pete," she murmured. "The longer we wait, the farther away the cattle are going to drift."

Pete turned his head to look at her, saw the silent pleading in her eyes and at last gave in to it. "Right," he muttered, and turned to flip the reins over the horse's head. He stuck a foot in the stirrup and swung up into the saddle. Though it chapped his butt to do so, he turned back to the wise-ass who'd called him Wyatt Earp. "If you don't mind, I'd appreciate it if you'd hook the trailer back up to my truck and drive it down the road to the break in the fence. Stretch it out across the highway to form a barricade, then set up flares a quarter of a mile or so farther up the highway to warn off any travelers, and in the opposite direction, as well.

"Meanwhile," he continued, "Carol and I'll ride back this way a bit," he said with a jerk of his chin toward her house, "and start herding the cattle toward the break." Spooked by the flashing lights and the sirens, Pete's horse began to prance nervously, tossing its head. He laid a hand against the horse's neck and rubbed, soothing the animal.

Firming his lips to keep from cussing a blue streak and telling the trooper what he could do with all his fancy technology, Pete turned his gaze to the trooper again, struggling to remain calm. "I'd really

appreciate it if you'd turn off those lights and sirens."

The Trooper frowned, hesitated a heart-stopping
moment, then turned. "Cut the lights," he yelled.
"And kill those sirens."

Almost instantly darkness fell over the area, the
only light remaining that offered by the moon shining overhead and the occasional bob of a flashlight's
beam.

"Thanks," Pete murmured, and reined his horse
around. "You take drag, Carol," he instructed as
she swung up into the saddle. "Dirt and I'll flank."
He put a finger and thumb between his teeth and let
out a shrill whistle. "Dirt! Heel!" The dog tore from
the scrub brush growing alongside the highway,
barking wildly, obviously enjoying this late-night
cattle drive.

Setting his jaw, Pete muttered, "Let's do it," and
spurred his horse toward the fence. Carol trailed
him, both of them following as close to the fence
line as possible to keep from stampeding the milling
cattle in the opposite direction.

"Dirt!" Pete yelled as he worked his lasso free
from the strips of leather that attached it to his saddle. Once he had the dog's attention, he pointed to
the opposite side of the highway and a steer that
trotted in the drainage ditch, headed in the wrong
direction. "Get him, boy!"

Dirt took off at a run, barking and nipping at the
steer's nose, turning the animal around. The steer
bawled miserably and broke into a run.

"Close in behind him, Carol," he yelled, "and
let's get these cattle movin'."

*   *   *

From the drag position behind the herd, Carol had a full view of Pete and Dirt working. The two quickly developed a rhythm, with Dirt chasing the cattle from the brush and Pete pushing them onto the highway and across it to join with the other cattle they'd gathered, already moving at a pretty fast clip down the opposite fence line. Carol's job was to keep the pressure on the cattle from the rear, in order to keep them moving, and chase the occasional animal that decided to break from the herd and run.

The work was tedious, exhausting, especially considering the added constraints of working at night and on different levels and types of ground, specifically the asphalt highway. When the trailer finally came into sight, its white steel pipes gleaming in the moonlight, she almost wept with relief.

"Dirt!" Pete yelled, loping along the highway's far shoulder. "Turn 'em!"

Dirt darted behind the herd and ran down the far side, streaking past Pete and barking furiously. He made a leap for the lead steer's nose, turning him toward the break in the fence.

Carol dug her boot heels into her horse's sides. "Get up, there!" she yelled, waving her arm and urging the cattle faster toward the break.

From the corner of her eye, she could see Pete loping along the shoulder, waving his lariat in the air, shooing the cattle toward the opening.

When the last steer ducked through the break in the barbed wire, Pete swung down from his horse and quickly tied the reins to a post. Jogging back up the incline to the highway and his truck, he manhandled a length of portable fencing from the truck's bed, then retraced his steps, more slowly this time, burdened by the weight of the steel fencing he carried.

Carol quickly dismounted, tied her horse and moved to help him.

"There's stray wire wrapped around that post," Pete said, breathing heavily. "Pull off a piece, and let's rig this sucker in place."

Carol found the wire and hurried back, wrapping the strand around the steel fencing and securing it to the post while Pete struggled to hold the portable fencing upright. When they'd secured both sides, Pete bent at the waist and grabbed his thighs, just above his knees, and squeezed, his chest heaving.

He glanced over his shoulder at the line of headlights that stretched down the highway a half mile or more in both directions. "Oh, Lord," he groaned. Straightening, he limped over to untie his horse.

"Pete?" Carol asked in concern, noticing his limp. "Did you hurt your knee?"

"Don't ask," he murmured wearily, and headed up the incline, leading his horse behind him. "If I don't think about, it can't hurt," he added grimly as he limped past her.

Nine

With the cattle back in the pasture and the horses unloaded and munching well-earned oats, Carol hesitated outside the barn, unsure how she was supposed to get back home.

Pete switched off the barn lights and stepped outside. He paused a moment, drawing in a deep breath, then slung an arm around her shoulders. "Come on up to the house and I'll buy you a beer."

Though the gesture was a friendly one, as was the offer of a beer, she could feel the weight he shifted to her shoulders as he headed her toward the house, limping noticeably at her side.

Though she was sure she would regret the action later, she slipped an arm around his waist to offer more support. "Your knee's hurting you again, isn't it?" she asked uncertainly.

"My knee *always* hurts," he reminded her. "That's a given."

She caught her lower lip between her teeth as she struggled to take more of his weight, remembering him saying that same thing to her before.

On the back porch she opened the kitchen door, then propped a hip against it, holding it open as she guided Pete inside. He grinned as she slipped from beneath his arm, bracing a hand against his back to help him inside.

"Do you feel as if we've danced this dance before?" he teased, looking over his shoulder at her.

She snorted a laugh and gave him a shove, pushing him across the threshold.

Once inside, he paused, his shoulders sagging wearily. "Thanks, Carol," he murmured. "I couldn't have done it without you."

"Oh, yes you could," she told him firmly, giving him another push. "And whatever you do, don't stop moving. If you do, I'm afraid I'll never get you going again."

He chuckled, the sound coming from deep in his chest as he limped down the long hall toward the master bedroom. At the doorway he stopped and braced his hands against the frame.

"Pete!" Carol cried, digging a shoulder into his back and pushing. "Don't stop now."

"I have to," he said, his voice low.

"Why?" she asked in surprise, straightening to stare at the back of his head.

He turned to look at her over his shoulder. "I'm afraid if I don't, you'll follow me inside, and once you do, I won't want you to leave again."

Carol took a step back, stunned by the need she saw in his eyes, in the desperation she heard in his voice. "Pete," she began hesitantly.

He held up a hand, interrupting her. "No, don't say it." He inhaled deeply then turned to stare at the bed. "Go home, Carol," he murmured. "Take Clayton's ranch truck and go home where you belong."

"But, Pete—"

"Go home, Carol," he repeated. "I'll be fine."

Carol stood before the kitchen window, gently swishing a sinkful of hand washables through the warm, sudsy water. Her gaze was on the hill beyond the kitchen window and the oak tree that grew there. Beneath it she could see the slab of granite that marked her son's grave.

Our son, she corrected. Pete's and my son.

Even as she made the silent amendment, she realized it was the first time she'd ever thought of their son in that way. Selfishly—even if it had been as a form of self-protection—she'd never allowed herself to think of her son in any way but as hers alone.

"Pete's and my son," she made herself say out loud.

Oddly, the sound of their names, joined by their son, brought her a measure of comfort, even pleasure. Suffering alone through the pregnancy, then through the loss of their baby, had been difficult for her. But now she felt as if she had someone to share the grief with, albeit separately.

She inhaled sharply, stopping the sudden rush of tears before they could rise. She wouldn't cry any-

more, she promised herself. She would only allow
herself to think of the good times, the good*ness* in
the man who had fathered her child.

And Pete was a good man, she reflected silently.
The fact that he'd willingly missed several rodeos,
endangering his rank in the standings, in order to
help out his friend was proof of that.

She smiled softly, thinking of Pete with Adam.
And he would have made a good daddy, she thought
wistfully, her gaze going to the granite stone up on
the hill. Pete had a huge heart and an enormous
sense of fun that any child would find hard to resist.

Too bad he didn't realize it, she thought sadly.

Giving herself a shake, she dipped her hands
deeply into the water and closed her fingers around
a blouse and squeezed. Too much work to be done
to waste time on daydreaming, she told herself. Lifting a shoulder, she brushed her cheek across it, wiping the tears, then sniffed.

She dipped her hands again and swished the
blouse through the water, watching the soap bubbles
form, then explode, shooting minuscule beads of
water and soap into the air to fall and settle again
over the clothes soaking in the sink. Sighing, she
lifted her face again to look out the window.

Startled, she straightened. "Pete?" she murmured
in bewilderment, watching him start up the hill,
limping beneath the weight of a thickly wrapped object he hefted on one shoulder.

Grabbing up a dish towel, she quickly dried her
hands, then tossed the towel aside as she hurried for
the back door. On the porch she paused, watching

his labored ascent, her heart nearly breaking at the severity of his limp.

He'd injured his knee again while rounding up Clayton's cattle, she thought, her heart going out to him. But he would probably choose a stomping by a rank bronc over admitting to the pain. She smiled softly at the thought, then gathered her brow in a frown as she wondered what on earth Pete was doing climbing her hill. And what was that he was carrying?

Her curiosity getting the better of her, she hurried down the steps and started up the hill just as Pete reached its summit, stopping beneath the old oak's wide-spread limbs. She quickened her step when he slowly sank to one knee and carefully lowered the object he carried to the ground. Her heart pounding, Carol broke into a run.

She came to a stop behind him and pressed a hand between her breasts, trying to catch her breath. "Pete?" she gasped. "What are you doing?"

He glanced behind him, only then aware of her presence, and frowned slightly as he turned back around. "I'm leaving, Carol," he murmured as he pulled the strings, untying the thick cord wrapped around the canvas.

Carol clapped her hands over her mouth to smother a sob.

"I was going to stop by the house before I left and tell you. But first I had this to do." Carefully, he folded back the canvas, exposing a stone, much like the one Carol had purchased for their son's small grave.

With her fingers still pressed tightly over her

mouth, Carol read the words inscribed on the smooth face of the granite.

> Infant son of Carol Benson and Pete Dugan
> July 16, 1998
> Gone, but never forgotten
> Your memory lives on
> in your parents' hearts.

Overcome with emotion at the words he'd added to those she'd originally had carved, Carol dropped to her knees behind Pete and wrapped her arms around him, pressing her cheek against his back. He lifted a hand and covered hers, holding her hands firmly against his chest. Beneath her palm she could feel the beat of his heart, the sigh of defeat that moved through him.

"I know that in your eyes I don't deserve a claim on our son," he said, his voice low and filled with regret. "But I want him to know that he was loved by both his parents, not just by one."

Choking on a sob, Carol buried her face against the warmth of his back.

He tightened his fingers over hers. "I just want to know one thing," he said, and turned within her embrace to face her. "Why did you bury him here?"

Carol looked up at him through a thick sheen of tears and saw the pain in his eyes, as well as the grief...and knew that she was responsible for it. Wanting to offer him comfort, but knowing she had no right after denying him the knowledge of their son, she drew her arms from around him and fisted her hands in her lap.

"Because this is where he was conceived. And because—" She paused and drew in a shuddering breath, digging deep for the courage to say it all. "And because this is the one spot where I felt he would most feel our love."

Pete stared at her, stunned to hear her acknowledge that he might have felt something for their son, other than regret for ever siring him. He inhaled deeply, trying not to hope, but finding it impossible to do anything else as he looked deeply into her eyes and finding nothing but honesty there. Reaching blindly for her hands, he gripped them between his own. "I do love him, Carol. I do." Even as he said the words, he knew them to be true. No man could feel this terrible pain, this rending within his heart, and not recognize the feeling as being that of a father's love for his son.

Choked by emotion, Carol tore her hands from his and threw her arms around his neck, clinging to him, wanting to comfort him, to reassure him. "He knows that, Pete," she whispered tearfully. "Somehow I know that our son knows that."

Her eyes squeezed tight to hold back the flood of tears that threatened, she felt his arms come around her. Unable to hold back the emotion any longer, she buried her face in the curve of his neck. "I'm so sorry that I didn't tell you about him from the beginning," she sobbed. "For robbing you of the opportunity to know him as I did—for causing you so much pain."

Feeling his arms tighten around her, the grief that trembled through him, she withdrew slightly and dragged her hands from around his neck to frame his face. Smiling up at him through her own tears, she gently thumbed away the moisture that dampened his lashes. "You'd have made a wonderful father, Pete," she told him. "The absolute best. And, if he'd lived, our son would have been proud to have you for his daddy."

Pete groaned and hauled her against his chest. "Oh, Carol," he murmured, burying his face in her hair. "That's what haunts me. That's what holds me back. I don't know if I'd be any good as a parent, or a husband, either, for that matter." He drew away to look at her. "What if I discovered that I was like my old man? Unwilling to accept the responsibilities that go along with having a family?" He dropped his arms from around her and sank back on his heels, digging his fists against his eyes. "I am like my father," he muttered miserably. "I know I am. There were times when I wanted to leave that house, the same as he did. Times when I couldn't stand to be in there and hear my mother cry."

"Oh, Pete," she said softly, pulling his fists from his eyes and gripping them within her hands. "Feeling that way isn't a sign of weakness or an indication of your inability to accept responsibility. It's a testament of your love for her, that you cared enough about her not to want her to suffer any longer. Leaving, removing *yourself* from the situation, was the only way you knew to end that suffering." She smiled up at him and gave his hands a reassuring squeeze. "You were young, Pete. No more than a boy. But you never left her. You took good care of your mother. I have no doubt about that. And you should never question that she felt your love. I'm sure that she did."

Sighing, he dipped his chin to his chest and opened his hands and curled his fingers around hers to grip them tightly within his own. He squeezed until her knuckles turned white. "Carol?" he said, lifting his face to look at her.

"Yes, Pete?"

"Do you love me?"

Her lips trembling, she smiled tenderly and lifted a hand to rest against his cheek. "Always."

He blew out a long breath. "Wow," he murmured.

Carol laughed, and rocked back on her heels. "Is that so hard to believe?"

He shook his head slowly, then grinned at her. "No, I guess not." He lifted a shoulder and added sheepishly, "I saw my picture on top of your TV set."

Her mouth dropped open upon hearing the confession. "Pete Dugan! What were you doing snooping around my house?"

"I wouldn't exactly call it snooping," he said in his defense.

Carol folded her arms across her breasts. "Well, what would you call it, then?"

He scrunched his mouth to one side, then snorted a laugh. "Snooping."

Rolling from his knees to sit on the grass, he tugged Carol onto his lap and wrapped his arms around her, hugging her back against his chest. He propped his chin on her shoulder and looked down at the stone. "Tell me about him," he said softly.

Carol reached a hand behind her to lay it against Pete's cheek. "He was beautiful," she said, remembering. "Perfect. With a mop of the blackest hair you've ever seen."

"Black?" he repeated in surprise, angling his head to peer at her. "Who'd he get that from?"

She lifted a shoulder as she smoothed her fingers down his cheek. "I don't know. But Clayton and Rena's twins had dark hair, too, when they were born, and look at them now. Both as blond as they can be."

He turned his gaze back to the stone and wrapped his arms tighter around her, drawing her closer against his chest, against his heart. "What happened to him?"

Carol sighed, feeling the loss all over again, the devastation. "The umbilical cord was wrapped around his neck. No one realized it until it was too late."

"He didn't suffer?"

"No," she assured him. "He didn't suffer."

They continued to sit there in the shade of the old oak tree with a light breeze rustling the leaves overhead, the song of a bird warbling high in the branches, undisturbed by the presence of the couple sitting on the cool grass below.

"Carol?"

"Hmmm?" she murmured, lulled by the comfort of the arms wrapped around her and the warmth of the body pressed against her back.

"Marry me."

She tensed, then twisted her head around to peer at him. "You're kidding? Right?"

"No, I'm serious."

"Oh, Pete," she said, sagging weakly.

"Now, before you start harping about roots and stability," he warned, "I'm going to tell you right now that I want the same damn thing."

Her eyes widened as she twisted around in his arms in order to better see him. "You do?"

"Yes, I most certainly do. And I want more children, too."

"Oh, Pete," she said, suddenly finding it hard to breathe. "Are you sure?"

"Never more sure about anything in my life. And I've been thinking about these horseback riding lessons you offer. Now if we were to—"

"Pete, I've already told you," she warned him. "How I run my business is *no* business of yours."

He just grinned. "You're thinking that I was going to fuss at you again for what you charge for those lessons, now weren't you?"

She pursed her lips. "Well, you were, weren't you?"

"As a matter of fact, I wasn't." He reared back to lie down on the grass, stretching out his legs, and drew her down beside him. Pillowing her head with one arm and crooking the other behind his own, he crossed his legs and stared up at the tangle of leaves overhead and the sky peeking through them. "Here's how I see it," he began. "We'll build us an arena right here, so we won't have to be running over to Clayton's all the time. And we can add more classes, maybe even a few clinics. And when my knee finally plays out, and I can't rodeo anymore, I figure I can start adding some classes of my own.

Might even build me a full rodeo arena, and hold some buck-outs right here on our own property. 'Course when the babies start coming—''

Carol pushed to an elbow and looked down at him, smiling, her eyes filled with her love for him. "Pete Dugan. I love you."

"'Course you do," he said, and hooked an arm behind her neck, pulling her down for a kiss. "What's not to love?"

She ground an elbow into his stomach, making him yelp. "You might try telling me that you love me, too," she said, pouting.

"Well, of course I love you," he cried. "I always have. And I sure as hell wouldn't have asked you to marry me if I didn't."

She settled down by his side again, satisfied, and snuggled close, closing her eyes. "Well, it's still nice to hear, every now and again."

Suddenly she was on her back, and Pete was stretching out on top of her, squeezing the breath from her lungs.

"I love you, I love you, I love you, I love you," he murmured, dropping kisses on first her eyes, then her cheeks, between each declaration of his love. When he'd completed the circle, he settled his mouth over hers, "Is that enough?" he whispered hopefully against her lips, then howled when she sank her teeth into his lower lip.

"No," she said haughtily, then soothed the spot she'd bitten with her tongue. "And if you're going to be difficult about this, Pete, then I'm just going to have to—''

He crushed his mouth over hers, thrusting his

tongue deeply inside and swirling it to mate with
hers. When he withdrew to look down at her, she
was breathing hard, her eyes wide and staring as she
looked up at him. ''You're going to have to what?''
he teased.

''It wasn't important,'' she said, and pulled his
face down to hers again. ''Not important, at all.''

* * * * *

Next month, look for

IN NAME ONLY,

*the next exciting book in
Peggy Moreland's new miniseries,*

TEXAS GROOMS.

*Available in August 2000 from
Silhouette Desire!*

*Here's a sneak preview of
IN NAME ONLY....*

Though it was almost dawn and the sky still clung to the colors of midnight, the street Troy drove his truck down was as bright as midday.

Las Vegas.

He gave his head a shake, then angled it a bit to steal a glance at the woman who slept in the passenger seat beside him. She sat with her head tipped against the window, her bare feet tucked up underneath her and hidden by her full, broomstick skirt. She looked so innocent in sleep, like an angel, and even more so than when she was awake, which was pretty darn angelic in Troy's estimation. Something told him, though, that this little angel's preacher daddy wasn't going to think too highly of a Las Vegas wedding for his daughter.

"Shelby?" he called softly, not wanting to startle her.

She shifted, snuggling a hand beneath her cheek, and a bare toe slipped from beneath the folds of her skirt, its nail painted a soft, shell-pink. As he watched, the toe curled as if inviting his touch.

Finding the sight oddly arousing—and himself more than a little tempted to accept the invitation and stroke a hand along that foot and up the smooth, bare leg beneath the skirt—he set his jaw and forced his gaze away. Clearing his throat, he tried not to think about that bare toe, or the stretch of leg attached to it, and attempted again to rouse her. "Shelby?"

"Hmmm?" she hummed sleepily.

"Better wake up. We're here."

Instantly alert, she straightened, slowly unwinding her legs and slipping her feet gracefully to the floor. Brushing her hair back from her face, she leaned forward to peer through the windshield. Her eyes grew wide at the sight that greeted her. "Oh, my stars," she murmured, darting her eyes from one side of the street to the other.

"Ever been to Las Vegas before?" Troy asked, unable to suppress the smile her shocked expression drew.

"No," she said, and turned to look at him.

"Welcome to the den of iniquity," he said, waving an expansive hand at the view before them.

Realizing that he had no idea where he was headed, Troy steered the truck onto a side street beside a hotel's entrance and stopped.

She peered through the window at the hotel's revolving door, then turned slowly to look at him. "Why are you stopping here?"

He saw the suspicion in her eyes. "'Cause I don't know where we're going, that's why," he reminded her. "Do you?"

"No," she said, her nervousness obvious. "But I'd think we'd need to find a chapel or something, wouldn't we? Not a hotel."

"That'd be my guess." He braced a hand against the steering wheel, inhaled deeply, then slowly released it, questioning again his sanity in allowing himself to be suckered into this crazy scheme of hers. "Are you sure you want to go through with this?"

She snapped her head around to peer at him, her eyes wider than before. "Yes! I have to."

"You don't *have* to," he reminded her. "You could always just tell your parents about the baby. They might be more understanding than you think."

"Oh, no," she said, frantically shaking her head. "My father would never understand. Never," she repeated in a hoarse whisper.

Troy sighed. "What about a friend, then? Surely there's someone you know who would agree to marry you."

"No," she said and shook her head again. "No one. Dunning is a small town. Everybody knows everybody." She lifted a shoulder. "And even if I did ask someone, everyone in town, my father included, would know the real reason for the marriage before the ink was dry on the marriage certificate. I won't subject my family to that embarrassment."

Sighing, Troy pushed open his door.

"Where are you going?" she cried, her eyes wide with alarm.

"I'm just going to step into that hotel there," he said, nodding toward it, "and see if they have some brochures on wedding chapels in the area. I'll be right back."

"I might just as well go with you," she murmured, glancing nervously around. "Might save us a little time."

Shaking his head, Troy took her by the elbow and guided her up the walk. An angel's first visit to Sodom and Gomorrah, he thought wryly. He wondered if she'd get soot on her wings.

Stepping back, he allowed Shelby to enter the revolving door first, then slipped into the compartment behind her, following as she stepped out into the ornately decorated hotel. He caught the gaping Shelby's elbow and quickly ushered her toward the rack of brochures. While she waited behind him, he selected several that advertised wedding chapels.

"How about this one?" he asked, holding up a brochure over his shoulder for her approval. When she didn't respond, he turned and his heart skipped a beat when he found she wasn't standing behind him. Sure that he'd lost her—or worse, someone had kidnapped her—he started walking, casting his gaze left and right, searching for her.

He found her not more than thirty feet away, standing in front of a slot machine.

"Damn, Shelby," he complained. "I thought I'd lost you."

She jumped, startled, then turned to look guiltily

up at him. "I'm sorry. But I've never seen a slot machine before and wanted to see how one works."

Unable to believe that anyone was *that* innocent, he dug a hand in his pocket and pulled out a quarter. "Here. Give it a try."

"What do I do?" she asked uncertainly.

"Just slip the quarter in that slot there," he said pointing, "then push the spin button. Or, if you want to do it the old-fashioned way, you can pull down the arm at the side of the machine."

He bit back a grin when he saw the way her fingers trembled as she dropped the coin into the slot. Bracing his hands on his thighs, he leaned forward as she pulled down the arm, putting his face on the same level with hers, then watched with her as the images flashed by. When the wheel stopped, three cherries were displayed. Immediately lights started flashing, the national anthem blared from a hidden speaker within the machine...and Troy gaped.

She jumped up from the stool, nearly knocking him down. "Did I do something wrong?" she asked, pressing herself against his side, trembling, as she stared in horror at the machine.

"Wrong?" Chuckling, Troy leaned over and punched the cash-out button, and tokens clinked musically as they began to spill into the payoff return. "You hit the jackpot."

"Jackpot?" she repeated, staring at him. Then her mouth dropped open, and she let out a squeal that had more than a few heads turning their way. Before he had a chance to brace himself, she threw herself into his arms. "Oh, Troy! That's marvelous! You won! You won!"

For a moment Troy could do nothing but hold on to her as she jumped up and down in his arms, painfully aware of the swell of her breasts chafing against his chest, the slender arms wrapped around his neck, her womanly scent. But then what she'd said slowly registered.

He'd won?

Before he could argue the point, she was whirling away and dropping to her knees to pick up coins from the floor as they spilled from the brimming payoff return. "Oh, my heavens, Troy!" she exclaimed, her eyes shining brighter than any star he'd ever seen light a night sky. "There must be hundreds of dollars here. Maybe thousands! You're rich!"

"That money's yours. You were the one behind the controls."

"Oh, no," she said. "It's yours. It was *your* quarter that I inserted into the machine. Not mine."

Troy stared at her a long moment, unable to believe what he was hearing. Any other woman would probably already be at the cashier's box, cashing in the tokens and thinking about a zillion ways to spend the money, not arguing over ownership. Shaking his head, he pulled off his cowboy hat. "An angel," he muttered under his breath as he stooped to scrape the mountain of coins into the crown of his hat. And a lucky angel, at that.

Peggy Moreland

presents three of the roughest,
toughest—sexiest—men in Texas in
her brand-new miniseries

Available in July 2000:

RIDE A WILD HEART

(Silhouette Desire® #1306)

Featuring Pete Dugan, a rodeo man who returns to
the woman he left behind—but never forgot!

Available in August 2000:

IN NAME ONLY

(Silhouette Desire® #1313)

Featuring Troy Jacobs, an honorable cowboy
conveniently wed to a pregnant beauty!

Available in September 2000:

SLOW WALTZ ACROSS TEXAS

(Silhouette Desire® #1315)

Featuring Clay Rankin, a husband determined to
find happily-ever-after with his runaway wife!

Only from

Silhouette®

Desire

Visit Silhouette at www.eHarlequin.com   SDTG

HONORABLE, LOYAL...AND DESTINED FOR LOVE

These are the **MEN** of Belle Terre

Bestselling author
BJ JAMES

brings you a new series in the tradition of her beloved *Black Watch* miniseries.

Look for the adventure to begin in August 2000 with **THE RETURN OF ADAMS CADE** (SD#1309)

And continue in December 2000 with **A SEASON FOR LOVE** (SD#1335)

Men of Belle Terre
only from

Available at your favorite retail outlet.

Visit Silhouette at www.eHarlequin.com   SDMBT

Look Who's Celebrating Our 20th Anniversary:

Celebrate 20 YEARS

"Twenty years of Silhouette! I can hardly believe it. Looking back on it, I find that my life and my books for Silhouette were inextricably intertwined.... Every Silhouette I wrote was a piece of my life. So, thank you, Silhouette, and may you have many more anniversaries."

—International bestselling author
Candace Camp

"I wish you continued success, Silhouette Books.... Thank you for giving me a chance to do what I love best in all the world."

—International bestselling author
Diana Palmer

"For twenty years Silhouette has thrilled us with love stories that ring true in the hearts and souls of millions of readers who know that happy endings are truly women's noblest goals. Way to go, Silhouette!"

—International bestselling author
Ann Major

Silhouette **Desire**

Visit Silhouette at www.eHarlequin.com.

PS20SDAQ2

Silhouette®

Desire

continues the captivating series
from bestselling author

Maureen Child

BACHELOR
BATTALION

**Defending their country is their duty;
love and marriage is their reward!**

**Don't miss the next three unforgettable books
in the series marching your way...**

THE LAST SANTINI VIRGIN
on sale August 2000 (SD #1312)

THE NEXT SANTINI BRIDE
on sale September 2000 (SD #1317)

MAROONED WITH A MARINE
on sale October 2000 (SD #1325)

Available at your favorite retail outlet.

Silhouette®

Where love comes alive™

Visit Silhouette at www.eHarlequin.com

SDBB3

If you enjoyed what you just read,
then we've got an offer you can't resist!

Take 2 bestselling love stories FREE!

Plus get a FREE surprise gift!

Clip this page and mail it to Silhouette Reader Service™

IN U.S.A.	IN CANADA
3010 Walden Ave.	P.O. Box 609
P.O. Box 1867	Fort Erie, Ontario
Buffalo, N.Y. 14240-1867	L2A 5X3

YES! Please send me 2 free Silhouette Desire® novels and my free surprise gift. Then send me 6 brand-new novels every month, which I will receive months before they're available in stores. In the U.S.A., bill me at the bargain price of $3.34 plus 25¢ delivery per book and applicable sales tax, if any*. In Canada, bill me at the bargain price of $3.74 plus 25¢ delivery per book and applicable taxes**. That's the complete price and a savings of at least 10% off the cover prices—what a great deal! I understand that accepting the 2 free books and gift places me under no obligation ever to buy any books. I can always return a shipment and cancel at any time. Even if I never buy another book from Silhouette, the 2 free books and gift are mine to keep forever. So why not take us up on our invitation. You'll be glad you did!

225 SEN C222
326 SEN C223

Name	(PLEASE PRINT)	
Address	Apt.#	
City	State/Prov.	Zip/Postal Code

* Terms and prices subject to change without notice. Sales tax applicable in N.Y.
** Canadian residents will be charged applicable provincial taxes and GST.
  All orders subject to approval. Offer limited to one per household.
  ® are registered trademarks of Harlequin Enterprises Limited.

DES00   ©1998 Harlequin Enterprises Limited

Silhouette®

where love comes alive—online...

Visit the *Author's Alcove*

➤ Find the most complete information anywhere on your favorite Silhouette author.

➤ Try your hand in the Writing Round Robin— contribute a chapter to an online book in the making.

Enter the *Reading Room*

➤ Experience an interactive novel—help determine the fate of a story being created now by one of your favorite authors.

➤ Join one of our reading groups and discuss your favorite book.

Drop into *Shop eHarlequin*

➤ Find the latest releases—read an excerpt or write a review for this month's Silhouette top sellers.

➤ Try out our amazing search feature—tell us your favorite theme, setting or time period and we'll find a book that's perfect for you.

All this and more available at

www.eHarlequin.com
on Women.com Networks

SEYRB1

EVERY WOMAN WANTS TO BE LOVED…

Join some of your favorite Silhouette Desire®
authors as they offer you breathtaking pleasure,
tumultuous passion and their most powerful,
provocative love stories to date!

July 2000
Ann Major
MIDNIGHT FANTASY
(SD# 1304)

August 2000
Cait London
TALLCHIEF: THE HOMECOMING
(SD# 1310)

September 2000
Jennifer Greene
ROCK SOLID
(SD# 1316)

October 2000
Anne Marie Winston
RANCHER'S PROPOSITION
(SD# 1322)

November 2000
Dixie Browning
THE VIRGIN AND THE VENGEFUL GROOM
(SD# 1331)

Available at your favorite retail outlet.

Silhouette®
Where love comes alive™

Visit Silhouette at www.eHarlequin.com   SDBODY

Silhouette® Desire

COMING NEXT MONTH

#1309 THE RETURN OF ADAMS CADE—BJ James
Man of the Month/Men of Belle Terre
An outcast from his home, Adams Cade had returned to Belle Terre to face his family—and his childhood love, Eden Claibourne. But when their reunion was threatened by Adams' past, could Eden convince him that his true home was in her arms?

#1310 TALLCHIEF: THE HOMECOMING—Cait London
Body & Soul/The Tallchiefs
The discovery of Liam Tallchief's heritage was still raw when sassy Michelle Farrell barreled into his life doing her best to unravel all his secrets. Michelle had never been a woman to stay in one place too long. So when Liam kissed her, why did she feel a fierce urge to claim *him?*

#1311 BRIDE OF FORTUNE—Leanne Banks
Fortune's Children: The Grooms
Accustomed to working with powerful men, Adele O'Neil instinctively knew that it would take a brave woman to get close to larger-than-life Jason Fortune. Could she be that woman? His touch must have jumbled her brain, because she was suddenly dreaming of home and hearth....

#1312 THE LAST SANTINI VIRGIN—Maureen Child
Bachelor Battalion
When Gunnery Sergeant Nick Paretti was ordered by his major to take dance lessons, he never expected his partner to be feisty virgin Gina Santini. And though the sparks flew when they were pressed cheek to cheek, Gina yearned for so much more. Could this gruff marine become Gina's partner—in marriage?

#1313 IN NAME ONLY—Peggy Moreland
Texas Grooms
Preacher's daughter Shelby Cannon needed a father for her unborn child—and rodeo cowboy Troy Jacobs was the perfect candidate. Only problem was, the two would have to be married in-name-only...and Troy was determined to make his temporary bride into his forever wife!

#1314 ONE SNOWBOUND WEEKEND...—Christy Lockhart
There was a snowstorm outside, a warm fire in his house, and Shane Masters's ex-wife was in front of him declaring her love. Shane knew that Angie had amnesia, but as they were trapped together for the weekend, he had only one choice—to invite her in and this time never let her go....

CMN0700